Mistaken Identity: Lime Peak Series Book 1

Forced Proximity, Strangers to Lovers, Grumpy Alpha Romance

This idea formed after I had my identity stolen ♡ Kitty Berry

Also by Kitty Berry

The Stone Series:
Sliding
Stoned
Siblings
Second Chances
Screen Play
Stealing Home
Surrender
Starting Over
Silence
Survivor
A Stone Family Christmas

The Anatomy of Love Trilogy:
Anatomy of Love (Anatomy of Love: Dr. Wilson Anderson)
Anatomy of Love (Dissection of Love: Dr. Caine Cabrera)
Anatomy of Love (Sutures of Love: Dr. Jessie Holt)
Vines of Ivy *(An AOL carry-over novel)*

Compatible Companions Trilogy:
You Are My Reason
My Forever Maybe

After You

Falls Village Collection
The Rest of Forever
From Then Until Forever
Promise Me Forever
Hard Promises to Keep
Forever to Go

Blossom Springs Duet

Burden of Proof

Romance Through the Year Novella Collection
A Slice of Sunshine
Bing, Bang, BOOM!
Tricked by a Treat
The Divorce Interlude
Late Bloomer
Whoopsie!
Kissed for a Cause

The Lime Peak Series:
Mistaken Identity
Finding Nirvana Sky

Contents

Blurb

Charlie Tyler likes order, consistency, and an unfaltering schedule. She's a tiny spitfire with a masculine name to match her badass personality. She's known in education as the queen of behaviorally challenged kids, but in her personal life, she's...wait, what personal life? Charlie can subdue the most oppositional defiant, troubled boys sent to Camp SubLime all while maintaining order as the camp's principal, but when it comes to dating men, she can't seem to do it right.

When a stranger comes to town, Charlie discovers a side of herself she hasn't been comfortable enough to explore. Could that be why her other relationships never worked out?

But Storm Roland is a challenge like none she's ever seen, and he's convinced the principal needs to learn a lesson only he's man enough to teach.

The undercover operative and financial wizard is successful at everything he does, so failure is never an option. Then he gets an assignment to bring down a drug smuggler disguised as the principal at a camp in Lime Peak, Maine.

But things are not as they seem, and as the two learn more about each other, they either need to side with the

school of trust or call things off and go with the camp of
protecting their hearts.

Storm

I haven't been in my new condo for more than a night when I get a call I don't want to answer any more than I'll want to deal with my twin brother when I tell him I'll be away for an unknown amount of time. Again. I just took over Corey's lease when he moved back into his house with his wife and kids.

Corey, my younger by thirty seconds brother, and his wife, just reunited and when he left his condo to move back in with his family, I gladly took over the lease with an option to buy. Now, I'll need Corey and Delaney to look after the place and my office until I return.

They think I'm still in the military, which is only sort of the truth. But it's the best I can do. I can't tell them I work for a private security firm staffed by a bunch of ex-military men from the most elite special force branches in the US — ANGLICO, Delta Force, MARSOC, and SEALs—gone rogue.

Sighing, I'm forced to swipe my finger across the screen to take my boss's call. "Mac," I say in greeting. "What do you need?"

"Hey, Storm. You free for the next couple weeks? Black said he spoke to you earlier, and you had nothing pressing coming up."

"Depends. You sending me to the tropics for some fun in the sun with hot pussy wrapped in barely visible bikinis?"

The once player turned family man laughs. "Lime Peak, Maine, but I hear they have an indoor water park with a few palm trees. I'll cover the admission for a day."

"Fuck you!" I scoff. "Maine? In February?"

"Yeah. Camp SubLime."

I laugh. "Doesn't sound remotely sublime to me. It sounds cold as shit, if I'm being honest. What's the job?"

"We've got reason to believe the principal at the camp for special needs kids isn't as wholesome as she seems."

Again, I'm made to laugh. "What's she doing? Running ADHD meds? Giving the PTA mommies some happy pills?"

"I'll send the file, but yeah, from what we know, she's running drugs for the cartels."

I nod, even though I know Mac can't see me. Drug running and cartels are his weakness because his father and half-brother ran one that almost cost him his life. It cost his partner and ex-girlfriend hers. And that's why he knows my answer before I speak.

"You can drive up tomorrow morning. Scope the place out, find lodging, then blend in with the locals. The camp should be pretty quiet for another week or two until the schools go on break, then the full staff and campers will show up."

"Who's there now?"

"The consistent full-time staff and faculty, the principal in question, and the full-time, live-in kids."

I sigh. "I'll look over the file and get back to you."

Mac chuckles. "I'll deposit your standard payment into your account. And thanks, man. Enjoy the snow."

The bastard chuckles again before he hangs up, and I groan at the thought of snow, slush, and ice.

As I knew they would, my brother and his wife insist I go there for dinner with my teenage niece and nephew before leaving for my assignment.

On my way, I make a stop at The Tipsy Pig, the only bar in my brother's upscale town, with a menu featuring pork inspired dishes and anything you can think of wrapped in bacon.

When Corey and my sister-in-law hit a rough patch in their marriage and my idiot brother fucked his young assistant while he and Delaney were on a break, he and I used to meet up there fairly often when he had the kids and had no idea how to make them a meal. The place has decent food, even better beer, and an endless supply of pussy on the weekend.

It's the latter that had me returning on the regular.

I pull into Corey and Delaney's driveway as another car is pulling out, and I smile and give the woman behind the wheel a friendly salute of my hand. Making my way inside, I find my nephew, Liam, and his girlfriend, Marley, hugging hello—that must have been her mom in the driveway, dropping her off—while Addison is watching some video featuring the Maine Titans.

The thought of them reminds me where I'll be headed in a few hours, and I make a mental note to pack my boots and heavy jacket.

"Hey," Liam calls out to me, then makes an announcement for the house. "Uncle Storm is the best. He brought food."

Lainey materializes and greets me with a hug. "You didn't have to bring anything."

I shrug. "I know, but it's their favorite. I figured you wouldn't mind an appetizer or two before dinner."

"Give it to me," she says. "I'll throw them on a plate. Your brother is in the shower, so he'll be down in a minute. Maybe hang in the family room and keep an eye on Liam."

I do as Lainey asks and wait with the kids for my brother to walk into the room with his hair still damp.

"Hey, man. You're really leaving in the morning?"

"Yeah. It should be a quick tour. Nothing too intense."

Corey and our younger brother, Rhodes, have been trying to talk me into retiring from the military for years now. I understand their points, which is why I had done just that about three years ago. But then Mac, my old CO, reached out and made me an offer I would have been a fool to turn down.

I spend my days in business casual, so taking out my camos every so often is a welcome change. But a parka and boots is another thing.

"You let Rhodes know to call me if he gets into any shit?"

"Yeah, he knows. Like I said, I shouldn't be gone long."

Corey smiles as Lainey comes in to call us to the table and snuggles under his arm. "Maybe this one can be the last. Your firm keeps you busy enough, and you're not getting any younger."

Later that night, after eating with my family and heading home, I finish packing, check my email for the information Mac has on this principal, and be sure I have the directions on my phone so I can head out first thing in the morning. The trip should take me about five hours, with a stop midmorning for food.

I open the principal's file on my phone and climb into my bed. It takes a minute to load, and I start with the written files, letting the photos take their time to download.

Charlene Tyler's file is boring at best. The youngest and only daughter in a family of six, she went to college and majored in education to follow in her father's footsteps. Figuring she was a daddy's girl, I'm not surprised she, not one of her older brothers, took on the administrative position upon her father's sudden death.

Her financials aren't any more interesting than her background. She's comfortable and lives within her means. No extravagant purchases or vacations, no over the top cars or needless toys.

I can't for the life of me figure out what makes anyone think this woman is running drugs for a cartel.

Callan Black, Mac's go-to man for anything and everything technology based, is a genius who, with a few clicks of his fingers, could complete a background check and have the information Mac is sending me into the snow to get.

It doesn't make sense.

Then I open the next file.

A maxed-out account from a pawn shop in the Bronx, an LLC for a construction company in Connecticut, endless bank accounts with cashed tax returns that are clearly fake, and that was only the tip of the iceberg. Mortgages, defaulted car loans, and major money spent on every outrageous purchase I hadn't found in the initial file.

It's as if she's leading two lives.

If I didn't know how meticulous Mac was, I'd question if he checked to see if she had an open identity theft case, but I know him better than that. I'm sure the information I'm looking at came from Callan, who also is a neurodivergent operative living not that far from the camp I'm heading to.

Again, none of this is making sense.

With the file of photos ready to download, I click on the first and suck in a deep breath when a picture of Charlene Tyler comes to life.

Jesus.

I know it's been a few weeks, and I'm used to sex way more often than that, but the fact my dick jumps in my pants at the first sight of this woman cannot be a good sign.

Okay, sure she's fucking smoking, but at my age, I should have better control of myself.

Charlene is a little whiff of a thing, but even in the pictures, she looks like a woman not to be messed with. I guess when you base your career on being the whisperer working with behaviorally challenged children, that was bound to happen, but I can't help but think about how that would translate into the bedroom.

Would she be dominant like she is in her career and edge me to the brink of insanity while riding my cock? Or are the pressures of her business life too much, and she likes to submit and let the man take her away, if only for a few hours of sexual bliss?

Shit! It doesn't matter because I can't find out. She's the woman I'm assigned to bring down in a blaze of glory in our fight against the drug lords and their cartels. She is not an option for my dick.

But...what I do here alone in my bed to get the idea of her out of my system is no one's business but my own.

I slide my finger along the screen, flipping through the pictures of her. Lots of them show her running on some sort of trail, a few have her smiling with her head thrown back and the column of her neck begging to be bitten. But my favorite—the one I land on to do the trick—is Charlene Tyler in a pair of tight yoga pants, glancing over her shoulder at the camera. Damn, this woman has a fine ass.

Her silky light brown hair is over one shoulder, and her lips are slightly parted. I can't help but picture the swollen head of my cock resting on that plump bottom lip of hers, prying them apart as she takes me into her mouth.

Her blue eyes hold me as I slide my pants over my hips and kick them to the foot of my bed.

My cock springs free, and I grip myself in my fist. "Oh," I groan at the tightness already forming in my balls, then I suck in a breath as I make myself hard.

Wrapping my fist around my steel length, I stroke a few more times. "Fucking hell," I mutter.

I allow my eyes to slide shut and I see her behind my closed lids. I watch her tiny hand move over the engorged head of my cock, then it slides down my shaft until it grasps my balls and tugs.

"Get on your fucking knees and open that pretty little mouth," I say in my head.

Staring up at me in my dream-like state, Charlene smirks and licks those pouty lips while my erection bobs an inch from her face. "Oh, I see. You're going to be a brat? That's how you want to play this? Tease me until I lose my fucking mind. Go 'head. Give it your best try, little girl. But you've been warned. When you play with the big boys..." I grasp the base of my cock for emphases. "You better be sure you can handle it."

"Oh, I can handle everything you've got," I hear her say in a soft, yet authoritative voice, husky and rough and so fucking sexy I can only pray for my sanity, her real voice is nothing like it.

I spit into my palm and rub it over my dick as I picture her there on her knees at my feet running her wicked tongue from my thick base all the way to the leaking tip. She then swirls it around in my pre-cum, moaning as she gets the first taste of me. "Mmm."

"You like that?"

She nods with my cock in her mouth, and I damn near drop my load right then.

Squeezing the head of my dick, I growl. This is not good, and I should stop this before it goes any further, but the aching in my balls must be relieved. I'll deal with the repercussions later.

Imagination Charlene groans and the vibrations shoot up my spine. "Holy fuck!" I swear.

Then I watch as her image in my head opens her lips wider to accommodate me as she tugs my cock all the way to the back of her throat with a deep swallow.

I can't fault myself for what happens next. After the time it's been since I blew a load, it's to be expected. And she's not real, so fucking her face with my hands gripping her hair and my cock making her gag, isn't a dick move.

"Motherfucker."

I ease up on myself because this dream is too good to let myself come already. But it won't be long before holding off becomes impossible, no matter how bad I'd like to savor this one experience, because I know it must be the last. Once I arrive in Lime Peak in a few hours, she's the bad guy and not a sexual option for me.

I watch as I imagine Charlene bobbing her head on my dick, coating me with her saliva as she gags again, a little less this time as she's getting accustomed to my size. "That's a good girl," I praise. "That's a good fucking girl, sucking my cock, choking on it." I sigh. "Man, I'm going to come."

My balls clench tight, and my shaft tightens to prepare for the explosion on the way.

Charlene senses my orgasm and smirks up at me from under her thick, curling eyelashes, her bright blue pools of innocence saying this isn't something she does, but I'm different. I made her do this. I made her lose the control she likes. Me. Only me.

She hums around me, and I grip my sheets. "Gonna come in that mouth and you're going to swallow like a good girl."

But she isn't a good girl. Nope. My dick springs free from her lips because Charlene Tyler is a little naughty fucking thing, and she thinks teasing me is fun.

I groan as I release my dick to ward off my climax, and I smirk to myself at the thought of this really happening. Her being a bad girl who needs to be taught a lesson over my knee. The scenario of student/teacher has potential with this woman, and I wish I could see where we could take it.

But I know this is only a fantasy and after I come, I can never think about her while I jack off again, much less have her in my bed for real.

But in my head, she releases my dick and my orgasm barrels away. "You are a brat, aren't you? Get my dick back in your mouth unless you want me to jerk off and come all over that gorgeous face."

She sticks her tongue out, flattening it in an invitation I'm all too glad to accept.

Placing the weight of my cock on her tongue, I wait for the sensations to pick back up.

My hand strokes my length as I watch her tongue run the path of a vein and sweat forms on my brow. Jesus, I need to fucking come.

Her lips are soft and pliant when she kisses my balls. Her bright red manicured fingertips are smooth when they tickle my taint, and my eyes roll to the back of my head. Then the vixen tugs on my sac, letting her talons sink in and I lose my breath.

"Oh, fuck yes, baby," I say as I pick up the pace of my hand and picture her sucking me back into the warm heat of her mouth.

I palm my balls in one hand while my other works frantically up and down my shaft. I'm definitely going to blow all over myself any second if I don't ease up.

But I do with a groan because I'm not ready to give up this fantasy with this sexy as fuck woman just yet.

"Fucking hell."

I thrash on my bed a little to take myself down a notch, but it does nothing to ease the growing ache in my balls that is now shooting up my dick.

I close my eyes and see her wicked grin.

"You evil, little thing," I state. "After I come, you're going to get your ass reddened so good, you won't be able to sit behind that desk of yours for a week."

Charlene pulls me back in, and I grip her hair in my fingers. "That's right. Suck that cock until I come. You're still getting punished, though."

She sucks fast, her lips squeezing me with the exact pressure I like, and I see stars. "Yes, oh, hell yeah. Don't you dare fucking stop until I come. You hear me?"

She sucks on my head with bruising pressure and the pinch of pain revs me even more. The sensations whirl through my system from my spine to my toes, then straight to my balls as they pull up tight once more. Then her hand grips them again in a gentle massage, her nails tickling this time before a lone finger makes its way between them and my ass.

"I'm about to lose my fucking mind, you dirty little girl. You want to put your finger there, go on," I encourage. "See what happens."

I'm not afraid of a little ass play in real life. I was before I tried it, but after I had my first orgasm from only having my prostate stimulated, I was a converted man. So, reaching for my favorite toy and lube, I imagine her spitting on her delicate finger.

As I slide the toy home, I arch off my bed and picture her evil stare on my most private place now filled with her finger.

"Now, who's the dirty one?" she asks.

I chuckle. I love a woman with sass in the bedroom even though she knows it won't end well for her.

"I can see we're going to need to teach you some manners and respect."

My hips thrust to meet her mouth and help to push me farther down her throat as the head of my dick tightens, and I know this time I'm not going to force myself to ward off the impending release.

My whole body grows taut as my balls tingle, and I sigh in relief as my dick explodes. Hot, thick strands cover my torso and drip from my fist as I shake through the climax.

Grunting, I refuse to let up on my cock even as my climax subsides because I picture Charlene Tyler refusing to let me go until she's certain she has wrung every drop from my body.

This woman has the potential to be a real problem for me, I can already tell, and I haven't even rolled into her life yet.

Finally, letting my dick go and removing my toy, I groan as I reach for a wad of tissues to clean myself off. Then I turn over and close my eyes so I can be up and out by six tomorrow. I need to arrive by lunch and get my bearings before I come face-to-face with the woman I just jerked off over.

Charlie

The sound of my heels clicking as I walk down the corridor is one of my favorite sounds. It will always make me think authoritarian thoughts, which is dangerous in this moment because I need to focus. I can't let my mind wander.

I clear my throat to refocus on my very prim and proper board of directors who I am giving a tour of Camp Sublime. The last thing I can think about right now is being a naughty little schoolgirl who is sent to the headmaster's office to learn her lesson over his knee. My luck, I'll blurt something out along those lines and regardless of my name, lose the only job my father ever wanted for me. The only thing I've ever done well enough to be proud of.

A few of my staff trail behind like a flock of geese flying south. If only a vacation in the warm heat of the sun was in the cards for any of us. Unfortunately, it's almost time to open the doors to the additional campers who have school vacations but their families can't or won't manage them in their homes. Instead, they pay for us to keep them for the week of their break while most of the parents fly off to one of those tropical islands us in education can only dream about.

I like my consistent staff and I can't wait for the few additional members to arrive who always bring new life to this place.

Named by my father, Camp SubLime—a play on words for the Maine town where it's located and the peace of mind we offer families—is a year-round live-in facility for children with special needs ranging from developmental disabilities to mental health challenges. Most of our residents are here twelve months of the year with a select few others joining us for their school breaks and/or summers.

Most days, this place makes me feel alive, happy, and fulfilled. Today was turning out *not* to be one of those days.

My morning started like every other weekday one did, with my phone easing me from sleep at the inspiring hour of five am. I stretched and jumped from my bed, ready to start the beautifully crisp winter morning with a brisk walk around the pond deep inside the trail at Flowerscent Gardens. I love sweeping my hair into an updo and changing into my sports bra and exercise clothes. My walking shoes make my calves look almost as good as any heel can. Then there's the glorious warm feeling of my muscles as I hit the three-mile mark.

Oh, who am I kidding?

I'm lying.

My phone wrenched me from sleep because I stayed up until after two finishing one of the hottest romance novels I've ever read, then tossed and turned while I thought about the sexy as fuck main character showing up in Lime Peak and crossing my path. It didn't take me more than a few minutes to yank my panties down and reach into the drawer of my bedside table for Zachary.

Yes, I named my vibrator, but in my defense, it's been a very long time since a real man has shown any interest in me, so it makes me feel better to think of him that way.

Anyway, I plunged into the romantic suspense storyline as my orgasm grew closer.

So the last thing I wanted to do this morning after only a little over two hours of sleep was change into a sports bra. I'm convinced the thing is trying to kill me one broken rib at a time. My walking shoes aren't much better. No matter how big I get them, they can't seem to not spring a hole where my big toe is. But it's oh so comfy to have it squeeze its way out while my muscles are on fire. And that isn't at the three-mile mark. That shit starts somewhere around my tenth step into the trail.

That's why instead of a sophisticated updo, I hit the path each morning with limp hair yanked into a ponytail that doesn't even bounce or sway from side to side.

While most of the other women I see, the ones who I'm sure don't need to name their sex toys—hell, if they have any, they're probably for their boyfriends to use on them—happily trot or full out run around the most gorgeous pond, I can barely make it out of the path at mile four without requiring medical attention.

But I do it with a smile every day, waving to passersby and pretending to enjoy a healthy lifestyle when, in reality, I do this so I can continue to eat my weight in chocolate every day.

Occupational hazard.

In most professions, people go outside for a cigarette break or develop a drug addiction. Teachers eat candy.

But I try to extract some joyfulness from the quiet of the park and the peacefulness it brings to the worrisome soul. It's my only chance during my hectic day to practice mindfulness.

And it is a beautiful, lush place, an oasis of green from the trees and the blue of the pond. Well, when it's not freezing and blanketed in white snow.

Anyway, it's a must if I don't want to hit meltdown levels of stress in front of my staff or the kids.

Those damn button-pressing kids.

And one of them decides now is the time to press one of them, which is why I said Camp SubLime makes me feel happy *most days*.

Not today because as we walk by Nicky Gillespie's room, he thinks it's funny to come and stand in his doorway, arm stretched over his head in nothing but a pair of tight, black boxer briefs and a vape between his lips. "Hey CT," he refers to me with the nickname the older boys—who couldn't act appropriate if their lives depended on it—gave me after one of our youngest students had an outburst one day and called me the four-letter C word. It didn't take the older boys long to come up with the nickname and play it off that they were my initials. That had nothing to do with it, and I knew it.

"Mr. Gillespie, you've been reminded we don't use initials when addressing faculty and staff, and I believe this will be your third and final warning about vaping. Get dressed and go see Mr. Lopez. Tell him I sent you."

I try to send a confident smile to the board members as I lead them away from the obstinate troublemaker in room eighteen with bipolar disorder and quickly text my assistant principal to expect Nicky within ten minutes, and if he didn't show to retrieve him from his room.

Rourke Lopez responds that he's on his way to get the boy, not even giving him the benefit of doubt.

I like the boy, I really do, but the disrespect I could do without.

Back when my father held my position, not one resident would have ever considered speaking to him that way. He was a fair man, but he punished harshly and ruled with fear.

I try my best to rule with fairness and offer the kids love and guidance.

Now, don't get me wrong. I'm not a pushover and Mr. Gillespie is in for a week's work of brutally hard labor every minute we're not required to educate or feed him. He'll be lucky to have six hours' sleep and showers for the next seven days. He can forget about free time or that pass home in two weeks.

The board follows me like interns on rounds with their attending, listening to me whip out quick orders to students who aren't where they belong, staff who thinks it's a good time to ask me a stupid question, or even one of them that makes a comment about the dorms being too warm and how we could save on our heating bill if we lowered it a few degrees.

When we return to the main building where my office is, I thank them for coming and dismiss them before they can ask another question about the budget, salaries, or the wait list. They came for a visit today because they want me to increase my staff's case loads and fill each dorm room with a minimum of two residents, so we'll have a full house.

All they see are the dollar signs.

All I see are more fights, less individualizing, and more faculty burnout.

Not happening on my watch.

"What the fuck?" Rourke asks when they leave because I called him late yesterday when I found out about their visit.

I shrug. "Money, what else?"

"Fuck them. Let them come and do this job for a fucking second and see if they think putting two or more kids who can't handle shit together is a good fucking idea. Never mind the raging hormones in this place with any of them over twelve."

I make a face.

Before I came to work here, I never worked with a child above second grade.

"What happened?"

Rourke drags his gaze up to meet my eyes and I know he knows something I don't, something he's hiding from me because he knew with the board being here this morning, it was the last thing I needed. "What makes you think something happened?"

I think for a moment, then drag my fingers through my hair, pull the tie from my wrist, and wrap it in a loose ponytail at the nape of my neck. "Because you knew the board was coming here today and you also know me well enough to know that's enough to push me over the edge. So if something, let's say maybe between teens in Black Bear and Lynx House happened after I left yesterday or before I arrived today, you would have handled it and hid it from me until you knew I wouldn't explode. You'd wait for the calm to settle back over me after my adrenaline rush from the board."

"Has that happened yet?"

"Shit! That bad?"

"Let's just say you were close, but instead of Lynx house, it's Mia from Otter House and Timmy Brown."

"She's sixteen!"

"Mmm, and Mr. Brown is eighteen."

I groan.

"It's not as bad as I'm sure you're picturing. Hands down the others' pants and at least they both know enough to give or deny consent. Timmy is a dick, but he wouldn't touch the girls from Deer House."

Deer House is the building for our live-in students with developmental disabilities without the capability to understand things like the consequences of sexual activities. In Deer House, we have girls from our youngest at five to our oldest at twenty-two. Seal House is the male counterpart.

For the most part, the residents of the other houses, those here because of their behavioral challenges or mental health issues, leave the residents from Deer and Seal Houses alone.

"Did you handle it, or should I expect a phone call from the innocent Mia's mommy?"

Rourke laughs from the pit of his stomach. Mia is anything but innocent. Her mother has her head in the sand, but the girl arrived here at fourteen bragging about her blowjob talents and the fact she held on to her virginity because she only had anal sex.

Yeah, it was a learning curve when I first arrived.

But that was three years ago, and nothing fazes me anymore. Not an angry five-year-old calling me a fucking cunt or a horny teenager with a detachment disorder having anal sex.

My phone rings and pulls me from Rourke.

"I'll let you take that," he says as he makes his way back to his office and I plop down into the chair behind my desk.

"Hello?"

"Is this Miss Tyler? Miss Charlene Tyler?" a strange, authoritative male voice asks.

"Um, yes. It's Charlie. Who's this?"

"Miss Tyler, this is Sergeant Buzzle from the Lime Peak PD. I'd like to speak with you in person."

"Oh, is everything okay?"

"Again, Miss Tyler, in person. I'll be here until my shift ends in two hours."

I stare down at my phone in disbelief. Did he just hang up on me?

Grabbing my purse, I head through the main office and stop at my secretary's desk.

Anita Jenkins is a no-nonsense woman who raised two daughters on her own after losing her first husband in a terrible accident when they were little. Anyone who knows anything about a school's dynamic, knows the person in her position is the real one in power. It's something I never let myself forget.

"Neet," I use her nickname. "I just got the weirdest call from the Lime Peak PD. Do you know a Sergeant Buzzle?"

Anita knows everyone in Lime Peak and the neighboring small towns of Waterland Isle and Falls Village. Her sister owns the only diner in the small-harbor town of Falls

Village—Mabel's Place—and shares the daily gossip with Anita. Anita in kind fills Mabel in on the school business she really shouldn't be sharing, but fighting that battle was a losing one. She never used names or said anything hurtful about any of the children, so if two aging ladies wanted to spill the tea every day after work at, well, Spill the Tea—another establishment in Falls Village—then who was I to stop them.

"If you mean Danny, then yes. He was a pain in the ass as a child. Grew up in Falls Village running around with that actor, Matthew James and his crew. Caused my sister hours of annoyance."

"Um, I guess that's him."

"What does he want? Someone turn in your wallet down there or something?"

"I don't know. All he said was he needed to see me in person."

Anita shrugs. "He was a prankster growing up, but I doubt they allow that nonsense from him at the PD. If he tries any of it, though, you go right ahead and do to him what you do to our boys here. You put his ass right in his place. Take a video for me. Mabel will love it."

Smiling at her sass, I tell her I'll be back as soon as I can and head to my car.

Sergeant Buzzle is exactly who Anita thought. A man in his mid to late thirties, decent enough looking, but I can tell a troublemaker when I see one, and he definitely caused his share in his younger days.

He ushers me into a tiny room and sits me at a table. Sitting across from me, he says, "Miss Tyler, you've been in Lime Peak for three years?"

"Um, yeah, give or take. What's this about?"

"And you live in the Cambridge Condo Complex?"

Many of my faculty lives in my condo complex. For as long as my father owned the camp, his staff lived there. It was sort of like our own camp, but for adults. We referred to it as the Triple C.

"Yes. Do you mind telling me—"

"When was the last time you left the country, Miss Tyler?"

"The country? I haven't left the area in months. I haven't been out of the country in years."

Buzzle looks up at me and studies my face to see if I'm lying. I know that's what he's doing because I do the same thing when I have a child in my office accused of some wrongdoing and I'm trying to decipher if they're the one lying to me or if the other party was.

He reaches for a file folder on the floor and tosses it on the table.

"What's this?"

"Your file."

I laugh a hearty sound because there really is no such thing as a file. I mean, sure, we keep our student's Individualized Education Plans in a software system, but the concept of a file that follows you throughout life, that just isn't a thing. "My file?" I ask. "And what exactly is in my file, Mr. Buzzle, and who, pray tell, told you to create one?"

The Sergeant smiles. "I was warned about you and your case of iron balls."

"Excuse me?" I stand.

"Sit down, Miss Tyler. We have reason to believe that either you are a drug smuggler for a foreign cartel, or someone has stolen your identity."

Storm

After finding the small town of Lime Peak didn't even have a cheap motel, I swung by the only realtor in the area and accepted a month's lease on a condo in the Cambridge Complex. It was literally the only place there was. Not ideal because I know it's where Charlene lives, but I figured maybe being close to her will pay off in the end. With my luck, we'll share a thin wall, and I'll be forced to listen to her fingering herself to orgasms every night while I'm trying never to think of her again the way I did before leaving New York. Not that that has happened yet. I already jerked off again thinking about the pictures from her file in my morning shower before hitting the road. I can't stop thinking about maybe doing it just one more time for good measure before I call it quits for good.

When I needed a place to stay last night, I called a few of the guys who live nearby and work for Mac. Not sure why none of them could have taken this job, but they're cool all the same.

Callan Black, Ace Lyons, and Elliot Montgomery are each living in marital bliss not far from Camp SubLime and Lime Peak, in a small town in Maine called Falls Village. Monte owns a restaurant and a bed-and-breakfast with his wife, Adams. From what

I can tell, Black spends his days in a tea and coffee shop eating his weight in pastries while Ace spends his remodeling his fixer upper.

The three are best friends and married to sisters, so their involvement in undercover operations has slowed down over the years.

Without a place to stay for the night—my condo wouldn't be inhabitable for a few more hours—Black let me crash at his castle in the sky. The town has two and par the course with the quirky guy, the other is owned by a man he still calls his nemesis, even though Ace and Elliot explain their relationship as more of a bromance.

Stretching, I decide to ignore my inflated dick and hop in the shower, where I continue to ignore it. Once dressed, I make my way to Black's kitchen, hoping to find the man so we can talk about the case.

Callan is a computer whiz and an all-around genius, which is why I'm having a hard time understanding how a few clicks of his fingers wouldn't give Mac the intel on Charlene he wants.

"Hey," I say when I spy him near the coffee machine.

"Hey. Jordan insisted I stay here until you leave."

"Oh. Shit, I'm sorry if I made her uncomfort—"

Black laughs. "Nothing makes that woman uncomfortable. She warned me I couldn't go to Colleen's for my breakfast because it would be rude to leave you here. So, let's go."

"Go?"

"Yeah, to Spill the Tea. They have better coffee than this thing makes and all the desserts you can eat."

"That's what you eat for breakfast every day?" I ask, wondering how he stays in top condition.

"Yeah. I stop back over there for my mid-afternoon treat, too."

I crack a smile. "I'm guessing there's a workout in between."

Black rolls his eyes. "Yeah, I don't want to be a fat ass. Let's go, I'm already late."

It only takes a few minutes for me to pack my stuff and load it into my truck so I can follow Black to his favorite local eatery. I want to head over to the condo from there so I can get settled in before the suspect arrives home from school. But first, I need to ask Black a few questions about the woman.

Sitting at the counter, Callan asks the owner, a pretty woman with blonde waves, for a sampler platter for me and his usual, which makes my platter look like a plate for a child. "You eat all that every day?"

"You should see what he gets in the afternoon," Colleen Walker says with mirth in her voice and an expression of fondness on her face for the operative.

After she leaves us with enough sugar to kill an elephant and the best cup of tea I've ever had, I turn to Black and whisper, "So Charlene Tyler? Why am I needed for this when you live right here and can easily get what Mac needs with a few clicks of your fingers?"

For a man trained in how to be a prisoner or war and not give anything away, his reaction speaks a thousand words. Black knows something I don't.

"I don't call the shots, just do what Mac says. Yeah, and I gotta run. Jordan gets mad when I'm not home for her to go to yoga with her sisters. Peace out, man."

Black rushes out of the shop so fast, Colleen reappears and confirms my suspicions when she says she's never seen him leave so early and with a few bites still on his plate.

I thank the shop owner and compliment her offerings with a promise to return, then I drive over to the condo complex and unload my bag.

Luckily, the unit came furnished and only takes a quick run to the home goods store in Waterland Isle to get sheets, towels, and a few cooking items. I make another stop at the local grocery store, then pick up a case of beer before I return home.

When I pull in, I spot a small SUV parked three spots down from mine that matches the car in my file for Charlene. With my cock springing to life at the thought of coming face to face with the woman from the picture who has been in the staring role of my spank bank, I decide blowing off some steam before going to her place and introducing myself as the new guy in town is called for.

I know from her file that Charlene likes order and was in the same place doing the same things day in and day out. That means she will be in her house relaxing after a long day at the camp, not on the trail she frequents first thing every morning.

With my running shoes and wearing the warmest workout gear I own, I take off in a jog through the complex to the entrance of Flowerscent Gardens.

The brisk air works its magic and keeps my mind from wandering to the woman I can't seem to get out of my head. The fresh Maine air fills my lungs as I pick up my pace and hit running speed as I make my way around a pond covered in ice and snow.

I pass a group of moms with babies in those running strollers Delaney used to put Liam and Addie in when they were little, and I offer a kind smile. Even with my earbuds in and on full volume, I hear a few feminine giggles and one asks the others if I'm new to town. Another commented that I must be because Lime Peak didn't make men that looked like me, whatever that meant.

A group of serious high school cross country kids fly around the pond and enter the wooded trail as a handful of workout maniacs are probably getting in their second exercise of the day.

I lower the volume of my music when I enter the woods so I can hear the sounds of the wildlife. Black-capped chickadees make their gargle noise, one of the most complex of the birds' calls, lasting only half a second. So catching it, I feel honored. Other animals are afoot, though, and I remind myself to be alert for moose, fox, and lynx.

The thought of Charlene out here alone in the early hours of the morning makes me wonder why she doesn't have a man in her life acting like an overprotective alpha-male. I don't even know this woman. She is so far off-limits, she shouldn't even be on my romantic radar, and yet, I'm feeling like a caveman over her.

I warn myself that a caveman can get burned by fire from a woman with the duplicity talents of a drug runner for a cartel.

On the far side of the pond, some young kids are having a late afternoon ice skating lesson while their moms film the action for their social media accounts.

And then, out of nowhere, I spot her.

Charlene Tyler.

Freezing my fingertips off—I didn't think to wear gloves for this run—I look around for a place to hide. As the sun sets and the temperature drops, the cold air stings, but it's worth it for the sight of her in tight joggers and a tight-fitting fleece. The top makes her tits look as plump as I imagined them while I thought about jerking off and coming all over them.

I duck behind a bush to watch her and not like a pervert staring at her amazing ass, even though I do that as well. But I gawk as she slows her pace and waves to the kids on the ice and their mothers who stand nearby. Charlene is clearly a people person.

She's shorter than I pictured, her steps small, but it doesn't slow her pace down. She's fast, actually. Very fast, and I quickly lose sight of her as she rounds the pond and enters the trail on the other side. Not familiar with the path, I decide to leave the cover of my bush and enter from a path behind me.

Not knowing if I'll pass her or not, I jog in a few yards, then when she still isn't in sight, I kick it up to a run until I see a patch of hot pink. Her sneakers, mittens, and headband that cover her ears stand out in the backdrop of nature.

Miss Tyler likes order, apparently. Little Miss Matchy-Match.

I duck behind a tree this time and wait for her to pass me. As soon as she does, I count to fifty, then take off in a run to catch up to her.

What my game plan is, I've no idea. Not as a man who wants this woman's attention nor an operative who knows better than to go into anything blindly. But here I am, running full force so I can run past her like some macho asshole and catch her eye.

But instead of that happening, I plow right into her back.

Umph!

Charlene hits the cold, frozen ground with a pained thud as the front of my body falls flat atop the back of hers.

My cock twitches in my running sweats and tries his best to notch himself in the crack of her perfect ass, but I quickly roll off her and groan. "Damn. I'm so sorry. Did I hurt you?"

I jump to my feet and tug her to hers.

She hasn't worked through the shock of being taken to the ground while apparently tying her shoe, but as soon as her mind works through that, I expect the flight or fight response to kick in. I mean, I can only hope this woman has the good sense to be apprehensive of a strange man my size, deep in the woods, who takes her to the ground with his weight.

Oomph!

Fuck! Yeah, so it's fight, then.

Charlene elbows me in the gut before I even see that coming, then her knee comes up and meets my balls in a punishing blow that takes me right back to the floor of the forest.

"I don't want to choose violence, but I will."

"Amphh," I moan. "That wasn't violence? Jesus, I'm scared to know what you think is. I'm sorry. I didn't mean to slam into you like that."

Her eyes roam my body, and I get to my feet again, bend in half and pray the pain shooting through my dick eases soon. At least it destroyed my hard-on. So there's that.

I slide my beanie off my head and use it to wipe the sweat from my face. Extending a hand, I introduce myself. "Um, I'm new to town. Just a few hours kind of new. Storm Roland is the name."

"How do I know you're not a crazy person or a rapist?"

I shrug. "I'm not, but you're smart to be cautious. I want to check you over for injuries, though. I must have hurt you."

She winces for the first time I'm seeing, probably because, like a child who falls and doesn't cry until they're asked if they're okay, Charlene is just registering the pain somewhere in her body.

I reach for her and run my hands over her knees first. Her pants are ripped there, and she's bleeding, so I know it's at least one source of her pain. "Shit! You cut your knees and I ripped your pants. Let's get out of this trail. It's getting dark, anyway. I'll check you over and we can exchange information so I can pay for the damages."

"No, no. You don't need to...oww," she cries as I grab her hand and realize her palms are scraped, too.

"God, you must think I'm such an asshole. I can't believe I literally plowed right into you."

She tries to wave me off and take some of the blame. "I should have moved to the side of the path to tie my shoe, but I'm scared to death of snakes. Speaking of, I think you're right about getting out of here before it gets any darker."

"Scared of bears, too?"

"I'd take my chances with a rapist over a bear."

"I assure you, I'm not a predator."

"Good to know," she says, then squeals when I lift her into my arms. "What are you doing?"

"Carrying you. What does it look like I'm doing?"

We reach the parking lot, and I pretend not to know I'm parked across from her, so I lead her to my truck. I have medical supplies anyway, and I doubt she does.

She quirks an eyebrow when I take out my medic bag. "Are you a doctor?"

"Nah, medic from my old days in the military. Now I spend them at a desk."

"Oh," she says, debating if she should share any of her personal information with me. In a small town such as Lime Peak, finding her from a few tidbits of information wouldn't be hard, even if I didn't already know everything about her. "I'm stuck behind one, too, most days."

"Really? You look more like the active type. With the late day run and all."

Charlene laughs loudly. "I'm pretty consistent in my schedule, but this morning I had to meet with my board of directors, then I got some disturbing news, so I came here to clear my head. Oh, and I hate to exercise. I honestly only do it so I won't die."

"Is that a possibility right now?" I ask with a smirk. "You don't look a day over eighty."

She smiles, and it lights up the darkening sky.

I get my supplies laid out, then wrap my hands around her waist and lift her to the open bed of my truck.

"Strange set of wheels for a guy behind a desk."

"Once a military man, always one. I'm sorry, but this is going to sting."

I pour some antiseptic onto a thick piece of gauze, then press it into one palm before I reach for her other hand and repeat the efforts. With Charlene holding the fabric to her hand wounds, I ask, "What's your name?" then tap another prepped gauze to her knee.

"Charlie."

"Hi, Charlie. That short for something or are you the only child of a dad who wanted a son?"

She smiles at first, then a wave a sadness passes over her features. "I have brothers, but they'd tell you I was a Daddy's girl. It's short for Charlene."

She meets my eye and offers me a sad smile.

"Pretty."

She blushes, and I'd give anything to make her cheeks turn pink like that every day of my life.

Shit!

"He died," she blurts. "Which made me principal of Camp SubLime. You probably drove past it on your way into town."

I nod, finish up the first aid, and jump up into the cab of my truck to sit beside her.

Stretching, I grab us each a water from my cooler. Handing one to her, I smile and say, "It's sealed, so no threat of me slipping you a roofie. What kind of camp is it, ski or something?"

Charlie taps the top of her water bottle to mine. "Not a ski camp. It's for kids with special needs ages three to twenty-two. Some live there, some just come for a week during their school break or the summers. Our preschoolers are local and only attend during the day. They don't live there."

"Don't you guys have schools here in Maine for that?"

Charlie chuckles. "Most of these kids have been asked to leave their schools for one reason or another."

Growing up, we had a neighbor who never came to our school. He rode a special bus, small and with an adult who used to walk to his door and hold his hand down the Johnson's walkway to the bus. Eric Johnson has a cognitive disability. Even at our ages now, he still lives with his parents back in the old neighborhood and can't be left home alone.

I tell Charlie about him, and she explains a child like Eric is only a tiny portion of their clientele. Most of the kids at

Camp SubLime are there because of their mental health issues and challenging behaviors.

By the time Charlie has schooled me in everything Camp SubLime, we're speaking in utter darkness.

"I should let you get home. It's late."

Looking at the screen of my phone, it's not all that late, just dark from the winter month we're in. "Yeah, I should unpack."

"Did you relocate?" she asks, and I shrug, not sure how I want to play that just yet. "There's not a lot of places around here. Falls Village, it's a town away, had a huge revitalization a few years back and ever since, real estate in this area is sparse."

"I'm renting a condo."

Charlene's eyes meet mine again. "Cambridge Condos?" she asks. "That's actually where I live. We call it the Triple C."

I offer her a wide smile. "Well, looks like we'll be seeing a lot of each other around the CCC, neighbor."

Charlie

Something nudges the back of my brain about the coincidence being too coincidental, but I can't seem to make it form a cohesive thought. I stress the importance to my staff about teaching stranger danger to our most vulnerable students, but here I am throwing out everything I know is good sense as I say, "Why don't you come over for dinner?"

Storm's face lights, but then he shakes his head and tries to protest because he feels guilty for knocking me down and doesn't want me to stand on my injured legs to cook us dinner. I turn down his offer of takeout and insist I'm good for making a meal for us in my kitchen.

He agrees to give me a few minutes to clean up and get ready before he comes over. So here I am with a towel wrapped around my head while I yank clothes out of drawers and hop around on my aching legs. Scrapping your knees really isn't something an adult should do. I certainly don't remember it being this painful as a child when I did it all the time trying to keep up with my daredevil older brothers.

I'm barely in the kitchen when Storm taps on my door.

Pulling it open, I catch my breath at his chin scruff and fight the urge to rub my legs together when I wonder just how good it would feel there. I take a deep inhale of his male scent and can't fight my eyes sliding shut.

Storm notices and smiles.

"You look like a genie in a bottle."

My hand goes to the top of my head, and I quickly tug the towel and free my limp hair. Shaking it with my fingers, I giggle. "Must have forgotten that."

Storm blinks then his eyes roam my body, and I can't stand still during his obvious and unashamed perusal. "I stopped to get this." He hands me a bottle of wine. "I didn't know what you were planning to make, so I went with red. I hope that's okay."

"I work in education. Anything that's wine is okay."

His jaw ticks. "Do you like your job?" he asks as I lead him further into my living room.

I shrug. "Yeah, I mean, I'm not sure if I'm cut out for this principal stuff, but I love the kids. The more challenging their behavior problems, the more I like them."

He nods, and I allow myself to process what a perfect specimen of a man he is. With a chiseled jaw and plump lips, the slight curve of his nose adds character to his otherwise perfect features. Storm is tall with arms and legs for days and muscles on top of more muscles. Running must be the tip of his workout iceberg. I bet he doesn't force himself to exercise every day the way I do.

"I have a teenage nephew and niece. They're not troubled in any real way other than being high drama for my brother and his wife. I don't know how you do it with an entire camp full of them. Liam and Addie are more than enough."

I smile. "Teens are the hardest. They're going through a lot of changes and trying to figure out who they are. They're trapped between wanting to stay little kids their parents take care of and wanting to be independent."

"That's a nice way of describing their chaos." Storm's eyes bounce around my place. "Your condo is so much nicer than mine."

I laugh. "I never asked you which unit you're in."

"Right next door."

Again, I get a zing of a warning, but it fades the minute I feel the warmth of his hand on my arm when my step falters. "Your knees sore?" he asks.

I clear my throat and take the bottle of wine from him as we enter the kitchen. "A little. I'll survive."

He goes back to apologizing mode, and I get another intoxicating whiff of his male scent when he comes up close behind me to look over my shoulder and see what I'm making us for dinner. I don't want him to ever move, but something makes me turn so quickly, he must not be prepared for it, and we end up bumping heads.

"Aww," I cry out.

"Jesus! I'm sorry...again. I'm not usually nervous like this with women."

A soft hum leaves me, and I ask, "I make *you* nervous?"

"Are you still considering me as a serial killer?"

I laugh. Am I? I think I've already decided that if he is, then I'm okay with it ending like this. I just hope he wants a good time before he does me in and he's not one of those creepy serial killers that like to kill their victims first then have sex with their corpse. There really is no fun in that.

Jesus, what the hell am I thinking? That I'm okay with this man killing me as long as we have sex first? Is this how pathetic I've become over the past three years since I've been at the camp and not dating?

And yes, by dating, I mean having sex. I have not had sex in three years.

Some slight movement of his has my eyes going to his hands, and even they are beautiful. Before I can stop myself, I reach for one and lift it. Turn it and study the girth of his fingers.

Oh, god, I bet two of them would feel so good inside me.

"Are you reading my palm?" he asks.

"No, I was just trying to see if you'd be good at cutting vegetables. Do you cook?"

Storm lets out a hearty laugh and raises his hands in front of his chest in defense. "If you count stopping at The Pig for bacon covered deliciousness, yes, I cook."

"The Pig?"

"It's this place, The Tipsy Pig, where my brother and I live. When he and his wife separated, he took his kids there a lot. It became our favorite place."

"Tell me more about the bacon wrapped around everything," I ask. "Even though I'm sure I should ask more about your family."

Storm tells me about the restaurant's menu while he chops the ends off the broccoli stalks and arranges them on the foil–covered baking pan I give him. I watch as the veins in his forearms dance when he lifts the bottle of olive oil and drizzles it over the crowns.

I can't stop myself from thinking of his crown drizzling over me.

God! I need to temper my inner slut down before I mount this man like a tree.

Storm is a sturdy man, strong with broad shoulders. I can't picture him happy in a suit behind a desk, even though that image was just saved into my spank bank for good use later tonight.

"So," I start. "Tell me what you do. You said something about the military but now working behind a desk. What brought you here?"

Storm shakes the seasonings I hand him over the vegetables while I start the water for the rice. "I went into the Army straight from high school. My brother wasn't thrilled. We're twins, by the way. And had done everything together until then, but Corey had zero interest in joining the Army with me. I did my time and made a career out of it while I also went to college, then got my MBA. I retired from the military a few years ago and opened my own financial advising firm in the town where Corey and Lainey live."

I pour the rice into the boiling water and set the timer, then take the tray of broccoli and set it in the hot oven to bake. "So, they worked things out?"

Storm looks at me quizzically for a moment and he looks like a teenager. A sexy as fuck, hulk of one, but still younger than I thought he was. I can't tell if this man is in his mid-twenties or his late thirties. Very diversified, this Storm Roland.

Who is he, really? I want to know more about him, which throws me because I don't remember the last time a man interested me enough to spend half the time I've already spent with Storm.

I prep the chicken and get it to cooking while he pours us some wine, puts crackers and pre-cut slices of cheese on a plate as I listen to him tell me about his twin's debacle with a divorce from his wife that never happened and how they are more in love than ever before.

In the light of my kitchen, Storm's hair is a dark shade of blonde, speckles of brown mixed in that us girls would pay a million dollars for, but ones I suspect are all the work of Mother Nature and good genes. Just as I'm trying to come up with the perfect color to describe his eyes—I was close to landing on Kermit green—he interrupts my inspection. "I'm not sure how long I'm here for. I have a few buddies in Falls Village, and they thought this area might be a good place for me to buy a vacation home. I work a lot of hours and I'm not good at relaxing where I work, so they talked me into checking it out. Elliot thought he had a room free, but Adams rented it, so I wound up here."

"Oh, you know Courtney and Elliot?"

His eyes widen and he nods. "Yeah, you?"

"Small town living at its best. Pretty much everyone in Falls Village, Waterland Isle, and here in Lime Peak all know one another somehow. I'm guessing you know Ace and Callan, too?"

Storm chuckles, nods, and meets my eyes.

"Don't look so surprised. We all know they do some undercover something or other. I'm guessing it's the military connection."

"That's confidential information, ma'am. If I told you that, I'd have to kill you," Storm says, pulling me to stand between his widespread legs. His smile warms. "I'm hoping you'll pick death by orgasm. That's my specialty."

Storm

What in the ever-loving fuck am I saying? What am I doing? I'm clearly not thinking if I'm honestly contemplating hooking up with Charlie.

First, it's a bad idea, and I know better. Second, Mac would have my balls. And third...I lose my train of thought on my aching balls when Charlie lets out the sweetest, flirtiest giggle I've ever heard as her gentle hands land on my chest.

"I know this isn't going to sound truthful, but I have really never, ever, not even once done this, but...um...do you maybe want to eat later?"

Catching her drift and not caring about anything else, I stand and throw my hands into her hair. A male growl, so deep it sounds like a black bear, rumbles through her condo as I walk her backward, our lips crashing together.

I land on the bench in her breakfast nook and take her into my lap, placing her warm pussy over my crotch.

Her eyes fly open when she feels my prominent hard-on, but they quickly close again when I run my tongue up the soft column of her neck.

"Charlie," I whisper into her ear. "You're so fucking sexy. Dinner can wait until breakfast because I don't plan on letting you up for air until."

"Storm." My name is a sigh, a plea, her way of begging for more, and I'm all too happy to oblige.

"Yeah, baby. Tell me."

She pulls back and meets my eyes. "I'm serious. I don't do hook-ups. I haven't had sex in over three years."

Well, that's a little cold water to the face.

"Um...okay. I...I'm not sure I know what I'm supposed to say to that."

She smiles. "Well, a guy that looks like you, I'm sure, hasn't gone three days without having sex. You don't need to lie to me. I'm a big girl. We can agree this is just sex and enjoy each other for the night. When we run into the other tomorrow, I won't be a stalker or a clinger."

I laugh. I've had my fair share of both, and I'm not looking for a repeat of either, but I'm aching so badly for Charlie, I'd damn near do anything to have her.

Her hands find my face and she pulls me in for another kiss. The taste of her fills my mouth and we smile into the embrace at the same time.

"Why are you smiling?" I ask.

"I don't know. This is fun." She shrugs. "You?"

I chuckle. "I'm about to get laid. That's really all it takes to make me a happy man."

Charlie is a small woman, but she's not lacking in the curves department. I bury my face between her ample tits and take in her sweet scent.

"Oh, god."

"Easy, Spunky. We're going to take our time. If it's been that long for you, we've got some work to do before we get to the good stuff. Why don't you get the oven turned off, then I'll get you turned on."

She giggles at the waggle of my eyes and my silly statement.

I like a woman who is fun in bed and doesn't take sex so seriously. Charlene is going to be a fun lay on top of having the potential to be a very satisfying one as well.

Fuck Mac, and what I know is right. My dick is in charge now, and I'll accept the fallout later.

I stand her on her feet and follow close behind her, my hands never leaving her soft hips as she makes her way to turn the stovetop and oven off.

"Lead the way," I say. "I want you on a soft surface and naked in the next three seconds, or I'll take any surface I can get while I tear your clothes off."

"Storm."

Her eyes dilate.

"Listen, I'm not going to hurt you, but I can already tell you like me being in control, so let me be honest with you. Sex with me will not be gentle. I like control, and I like my women compliant. I'm also not afraid to punish one if they refuse to cooperate. A strong woman like you, in charge of an entire school—"

"I don't want to be in control in bed." She shakes her head. "Not tonight. Not with you. I want you to take me out of my head, take my control away. Make me be a good girl."

"Fuck." I draw the word out and lift her, fireman style, over my shoulder and plow toward where I assume by the layout of my new place is her bedroom.

Storming through her bedroom door, I stop short at the fluorescent light of her enormous fish tank. It's beautiful, full of colorful fish and coral.

"Wow!" I exclaim, Charlie still on my shoulder. "That's amazing."

"They were my dad's. I couldn't give them up. It was a hobby he shared with me as a kid and when he passed and I bought this place, I had it transported here."

I toss her on the bed and follow her to the mattress. "I want to hear all about it...after a few orgasms. Now, about the getting naked. Your choice. You taking these off, or would you like me to start ripping?"

She wraps her arms around my waist as I catch her lips under mine. Our kiss is instantly urgent, all dueling tongues clashing and teeth crashing. When I feel the scrape of her nails at the back of my neck, I growl her name.

"I want you," she states. "Please, Storm."

"I know, Spunky. But we're going to take our time. And remember, who's in charge?"

She swallows. "You."

"That's right. Now these clothes."

I bring my palms to the sweet globes of her ass and tug her tight to my body, grinding my erection against her, so she'll understand why we need to go at the pace I set.

Charlie moans and shifts under me, making her sweet pussy come into contact with my bulge. I rock against her core, then quickly pull back, reach behind my head, and yank my shirt over it.

"Holy hell," she exclaims. "Holy hell, Storm. Are you serious?"

"I'm glad you like what you see. Now it's my turn."

She was warned more times than I'm used to allowing, and my patience is done.

I grasp her t-shirt in my hands and make one quick pulling motion. Ripping it in two, her breasts, clad in a white bra, become visible.

Charlie gasps. "You ripped my shirt."

"I'm guessing you understand behavior modification."

She nods.

"How many times do you tell your students you're going to do something before actually doing it?"

Her eyes meet mine.

"Exactly. I gave you more chances than I should have. Now, either take the bra off, or I will."

She shudders, but her hands make to unhook the back clasp in no time and her glorious tits spill into my waiting palms.

I capture a nipple in my mouth, and I squeeze her ass to feel the friction I'm desperate for.

But it's not enough.

"Get rid of the pants," I demand. "Now."

Charlie is quick to move now that she knows I'm a man of my word.

I watch her as she slides her yoga pants down her legs, but then I become impatient and rip them off her feet. Tossing them to the floor, I bury my face in her panties and inhale with a pained groan. "Jesus, you smell good, and these panties are soaked. You wet for me already?"

A small nod as her cheeks turn pink isn't going to cut it for me.

"Tell me," I order. "Say it."

She clears her throat. "I'm wet for you, Storm. I want you."

After ghosting my hand over her mound, I leisurely run a finger down her slit, over her panties. "Good girl."

Her eyes are hooded and those evil lips of hers slightly part at the praise. The thought of her liking it as much as I do makes my cock burn for her.

I want to be inside her so badly, I can't think.

I hook my fingers under the thin scrap of fabric covering her pussy and say, "I'm ripping these off now unless you tell me to stop."

"Don't stop. Please."

I yank them down, free them from her body, then toss them to the floor. "Oh, fuck, baby. Look how slick you are. Do you want my fingers?" I ask as I squeeze my raging erection through my pants. "My mouth, or maybe both? Open your legs for me and watch. No closing your eyes, no looking away."

She watches me with rapt amazement as I stroke my dick through my pants, then her eyes grow wider when I place a palm on each of her inner thighs and spread them wide because she still hasn't. "We need to work on your obedience."

Her eyes fly to mine, and I can't read what's behind them. A flash of defiance, gumption, and a little vinegar, if I had to guess.

"If you want to see the cock that your mouth is watering for—" She opens her mouth to speak, but I silence her with a finger pushing between her lips. "I see you looking. You can look all you want. It'll be all yours in a second if you be a good girl. Now watch while I make you come for me on demand."

"Storm, I...I can't come—"

"If you're under some misconception that you can't come from oral because every other guy who's gone down on you has obviously been clueless, I assure you, I know where and how to lick you, Charlie."

"No, I've never come with a man before, ever. No matter what he did."

I chuckle. "Even better. I like the challenge. Let's have you count each time I make you come. My money is on about eight before I leave in the morning."

"Eight?" she asks, then moans when I drag my forefinger through her drenched slit before I circle around her clit, careful not to give it the full attention it needs just yet.

"Open these legs wider," I command. "And if you're a good girl and come for me when I ask for it, I'll let you take my dick out."

I swirl my finger at her entrance and collect her arousal before adding a second, then bringing them both back to her clit.

Charlie lifts her hips, begging for more.

"Ask like a good girl if you want my mouth."

"Yes," she pleads. "Lick me."

I smile and lick her lower belly, right above her pussy. "Here?"

"No. Oh, god. Please."

"Tell me."

"Lick my pussy," she cries when I run my tongue around her clit.

Charlie's hands go into my hair, and she tugs me closer to where she is desperate to have me.

I lean into her, and trail kisses up and down her slit, moaning when I feel her arousal wet my lips. Sitting back on my haunches, I lick them as she watches, then I lower the waistband of my sweats and reveal the deep purple head of my aching cock.

Her breath catches when I part her puffy folds and lave her sweetness with my flattened tongue.

"Oh!"

I don't stop to ask what that sound is about. I know it's shock because her pussy tightens and pulses when I give her one, then two thick fingers right before I attack her clit.

"Now be my good girl, and come for me," I say and damn if she doesn't burst into motherfucking flames for me.

She's the sweetest taste I've ever had on my tongue. Like strawberries and something just Charlie. She's all woman and tonight, she's all mine.

I pump my fingers while she climaxes around them, my tongue flicking back and forth over her clit as she screams my name and arches off her bed.

I don't ease up when I feel her hit the crescendo of her orgasm. Instead, I lap at her pussy like a desperate man, tasting her flavor and savoring her scent.

Charlie lets me stroke her sensitive flesh with my fingers until I feel her climbing again.

"I think I told you to count," I warn.

"There's no way I'm going to—"

"Come again for me," I demand, then suck her clit into my mouth at the same time I push a finger into her wet cunt and curl it upward. It only takes one flick at her tender spot and Charlie breaks apart for me.

"Two," she howls as her body spasms so hard the bed shakes and smacks against her wall.

Perfect.

She's perfect.

But then I remember she's not perfect at all.

She's a suspected criminal.

What the fuck am I doing? Am I really about to fuck a woman who might run drugs out of a camp designed for kids with special needs?

I have to get out of here and get my shit together.

Luckily, Callan Black either has the best or the worst timing in the world.

Charlie

I try my best to wear my poker face to Camp SubLime the following morning, but I'm still drunk from the multiple orgasms Storm gave me. My head is spinning from the whiplash his abrupt exit caused when I walk into the Thursday morning staff meeting.

I was so distracted at the copy machine, Anita had to deal with the paper jam I caused and threatened to take my privileges away. Anita locks the machine. Without your individualized—hey, that's what special education is all about, isn't it? — code, you can't use the copier. She did this so she'll know who didn't pay attention to her lesson on proper use, and she can give them a refresher course...and hell for giving her more work.

By the time I run into Rouke coming out of his office with our weekly box of treats from Spill the Tea, I'm so on edge and jumpy, I bump into him and knock the goodies to the floor. His partner is a neurosurgeon, so of course, my bestie insists I need an MRI to check for a tumor wreaking havoc on my motor skills. I lie and tell him I'll get a PT consult later in the day to get him off my back.

But he's on to me and now, as I fumble to get my laptop and projector to get along, I feel him and Emily Carter staring my way. The young school psychologist is dating

Luke, a cardiothoracic surgeon from the same hospital where Rourke's husband, Brad, works.

Before I have time to ask one of the new teachers—most of them know next to nothing about managing or teaching children when they walk through our doors, but they know their way around technology—to give me a hand, Anita's voice sounds over the announcement system warning everyone to "get their asses into the media center in two point three seconds."

I wave off my head teacher in the preschool when she asks if I need a hug. Her assistants are with her and those three live on drama. I'm not giving them something to fixate on.

Finally, with my agenda on screen, I call the meeting to order with a clearing of my throat and a few fiddles of a pen I shouldn't need.

I know how much the staff hates writing their professional goals—they're right to think it's busy work, but the board requires it—so I don't dawdle over SLOs and IEGs. It's not a topic I love to discuss either, and with my brain filled with not much else other than a certain man and what he did to my body last night, my focusing abilities are shit.

I adjourn the meeting with one of my standards. "Get ready for another day in the trenches. If you think today will be better than yesterday, you're nuts. If you think you know more than the hellions you're in charge of, you're wrong. Good luck!" It's the best I can muster in the moment as a pep talk. Rourke insists I need to hire a motivational speaker to give my speeches a tweak. He isn't wrong.

"What the fuck was that?" Rourke asks. "Why would you tell them they're nuts and wrong? All that's going to do is get one of them to file for a mental health break."

I roll my eyes. Maybe that's what I need.

Obviously, it is because the next words I blurt prove I've lost my mind. "I met a man yesterday."

"My favorite five words," Rourke says with a waggle of his brows.

"What is?" Sally, our art therapist and a good friend of ours, asks when she joins us at the laptop I'm trying to disconnect from the projector.

"Charlie here met a man yesterday. That would explain why she can't motor plan today. Her body isn't used to attention, and I'm betting she got some good attention."

"You hooked up with a guy?" Emily whisper-yells, and I slap a hand over her mouth.

"Keep your voice down. I can't let the first-year teachers know I'm a human being with feelings. Are you crazy? They'd never hand in another lesson plan again."

As the commotion picks up, Ian, Rourke's brother and adaptive PE teacher, joins us. "What are you yelling about over here?"

"Charlie met a guy," Sally overshares and slides under her boyfriend's arm. Yeah, it took us some getting used to, but Sally and Ian are good together, so we only tortured them for a few weeks after we found out they were sneaking around behind our backs.

"Wait, like a real guy?" Ian asks. "You're not talking about one of those toys again, right?" he asks with a shiver.

"Can we not?" I beg. "I told you, what's in the drawer next to my bed is nobody's concern."

"Well, it is when I think it's where the fish food is and I find a big, black—"

"Black?" Rourke scream-laughs. "You never said it was black."

"Ribbed, too, like with veins. Damn thing looks real as fuck."

"Hey!" I shout. "They were out of the pink ones, and I had a gift card from my birthday."

The people I no longer consider my friends laugh at my expense.

"Back to the guy," Ian redirects the conversation. "I'm serious. This is an actual man?"

"It hasn't been that long," I defend.

Emily chuckles. "You haven't been with anyone since we met you three years ago. Just the other day you were crying the lyrics to that Rent song about the hours since you've had sex."

"Well, one million five hundred seventy-six thousand eight hundred minutes is a long time."

"How long did that math take her?" Rourke asks.

"Shut up. I had too much cheap wine."

"Okay, can we get back to this real guy you met.?" Ian asks. "There's not a lot of us roaming around these parts, so if you actually spoke to one, like used your words the way they say in the preschool, not just pretended in your head like you do when we're out and you see a guy but are too worried he'll know who you are and what you do so you pretend to have a whole conversation with him in your head then leave alone, I want to know who it is."

"I did that once. Okay, maybe three times. But having a vivid imagination is good."

"When you talked to this mystery man, did you gain his attention first? You know what we teach the little ones. You tapped him on the shoulder, made eye contact, and used his name?" Emily asks, proud of her social skills curriculum.

"I'm not a socially impaired child! Jesus, is this how bad you think I am?"

"Well..." they hedge collectively, drawing the word out.

"You know what?" I say as I finally rip the cord out of the projector and slam the top to the laptop. "If this is how you're going to be, fine. I'm not telling you about Storm." I walk out of the room, and I now have my entourage following me through the hall as I say his name.

"Storm?" Kayley, the school nurse, asks as we pass her, and she joins our conversation I am no longer interested in having.

I need to be careful with the details here. I've already told them too much by sharing his name. It wouldn't be long before they met him around the complex. With a name like Storm, I'm sure there isn't another who just moved into our small town.

"Yes," I state with confidence I don't feel. "You'll probably run into him soon, too. He just moved into the complex."

"Is he a teacher?" Kayley wonders.

I huff. "Not everyone who lives where we do works here."

"Most," Kayley says, and I shoot her a glare.

She is right. Our condo complex is the live-in version of the camp, but for the teachers and staff.

"If he's not a teacher, how'd you meet him?" Kayley just can't let this go about him being a teacher.

"I do speak to those not in education, you know? And if this is that important to all of you, fine. We met on the trail."

We're now in the main office, so Anita takes her turn at Charlie bashing. "If I'm picking up on this correctly, you met a man while dragging ass on the trail?" She laughs. "That's classic."

I glare her way now. Honestly, when did my staff lose all respect for me? Did they ever have any?

"Yes, I bumped into him there."

I walk into my office and try to shut my door, but of course, this group of so-called friends of mine push their way through.

I lift my eyes to them as I plop down in my chair. "Do you not have children to teach, jobs to do?"

Rourke is the first to answer. "Not that are more important than this. That comment you made. 'Bumped into' doesn't sound right. What happened, exactly?"

I huff out an exhausted breath. "Fine. I was running—" the room erupts in laughter, and I roll my eyes at them. "Okay, maybe it was more of a jog—"

"Trot, at best," Anita scoffs, and I growl.

"That's not even the point. I was bending down, tying my shoe when he came out of nowhere and plowed into me."

Another eruption of laughter fills my office, and I reach into my mini fridge for a water. Opening the cap, I take a gulp as the crew around me takes their time finding humor at my expense. Well, the laugh's on them because I'm not offering them any reasons.

"The plowing into her from behind while her ass was up in the air must have been a sight," Rourke says.

"Hey, it's how you like it," his brother teases him.

"You're one to talk," Sally adds, revealing more about Ian than any of us care to know.

"I admit it wasn't my finest hour, but you're acting like we were naked and there was penetration on this trail."

"Was there penetration at any point?" Anita asks.

"I'm not answering that!"

"That's a hard no, poor thing." Anita touches my arm. "Story just got boring. I'm going back to my desk. One of the little shits is bound to do something better than this any minute now."

"Mmm." I hum. "Especially if half my teaching staff is in here."

"How hard did he 'bump' into you?" Rourke asks. "Like do you think he really saw you, but used it as an opportunity to ram his junk into you from behind?"

"I'd ask how you were raised if I wasn't there." Ian chuckles. "But, seriously, Charlie, was this guy like stalking you on the trail? Was it dark out?"

I sigh. "It got dark as we talked. After he knocked me over, he carried me out of the trail because my knees hurt from the scrapes."

The group looks between themselves a few times before all eyes land on me.

"You probably should have called the police to be safe. You know that trail is no place for a woman after dark," Kayley says.

With a roll of my eyes, I say, "This is Lime Peak, Maine, not some big city metropolis. Anyway, he's a nice guy. But speaking of the police, I got a call from Dan Buzzle yesterday. He's the Sergeant. That's why I was on the trail in the first place."

They know I'm nothing if not consistent with my daily schedule, but with the board touring the camp yesterday, it would have been a day I normally skipped my run—jog, trot, whatever. But after hearing what Sergeant Buzzle had called me about, I needed some stress relief.

"He's a douche," Kayley says with a twirl of her hair, then her fingers come together to show about three inches. "And not worth a woman's time."

Ian and Rourke uncomfortably shift in their pants.

"Stop it," Sally says to Ian, and she spreads her hands a good eight to nine inches apart. "You've got nothing to worry about, and we all know how genetics work." She turns to Rourke and offers a knowing wink.

I cringe. "Didn't need any of those visuals, but thanks."

"Why did he call you?" Emily asks.

I walk them through our conversation from yesterday when I learned my identity was stolen. Somehow, someone was able to get every piece of my personal identification, including my social security number. When I asked Dan how he thought it could have happened, he said it's usually not from what I thought. I'd assumed I bought something on a fishy website or gave my information unknowingly on social media or something. Dan said it's usually a breech on a site like a hospital, an insurance provider, or a loan agency.

A quick search through my emails proved the latter to probably be the culprit. I had an email from six months ago from the agency my student loans were through informing me that there was a breech in their system, and I could have free fraud protection for a year.

Oh well.

Dan walked me through a bunch of steps to take, but in all honesty, he said most of them would be for nothing. So instead of doing anything, I grabbed my running shoes, and the rest is history.

"Wait," Sally stops me as I continue to ramble on about the fraud protection program in hopes of them forgetting about my male encounter on the trail. "Enough about that crap. I want to hear about this man who plowed into your ass."

I spit out my sip of water. "When you say it like that, it sounds like we—"

"Don't knock it until you try, babe!" Rourke says.

"There's nothing more to tell. He's our neighbor. I did the polite thing—"

"After he plowed you in the ass." This is said through a laugh from Emily.

I glower at Rourke because he's to blame for me being friends with this group. When I first started here, I wanted to remain professional. He talked me into friending this motley crew.

Reiterating what I was trying to communicate, I say, "I did the polite thing and invited him over for dinner. He brought me a nice bottle of wine and helped me cut up broccoli."

"Oh, my god! Did you sleep with him?" Sally asks, phone in hand, so I mentally count down from ten and wait for my office door to swing open.

And in three, two—

Right on cue, Sally's best friend, my music therapist, Shana Roberts, comes flying in. "Charlie slept with someone?"

I fling my hands up in the air and tip myself back in my chair. "Instead of shouting that through the halls, why don't you just ask Neet to include that in today's morning announcements?"

"That's not appropriate, Charlie. Don't be ridiculous. The students don't even see you as human. The last thing any of them care about is your sex life."

"But you're all up in my business. And by the way, I didn't sleep with him. Like exactly."

Emily goes to leave and says, "I'm going to pop into my office really quick for my copy of the DSM to see what we can label you as. Something is definitely off with you."

Finally, Rourke comes to my defense and wraps a comforting arm around my shoulder. "Okay, I think our fearless leader has had enough of our teasing. Let's let her tell us what exactly happened with her and the ass plower without interrupting.

He hands me the toy microphone I keep on my desk for when I need to engage in peer mediation with two or more of the students. Whoever is holding the toy gets to speak and everyone else has to be silent.

Amazingly, it works with this group of semi-adults, too.

Holding the microphone, I do my best to report the story without too much detail before the bell rings. But by the time I'm alone in my office trying to figure out how Storm and I went from me coming around his fingers and in his mouth to him saying he needed to take the call he got and leaving, I'm more confused than before.

Storm

I spent the night tossing and turning in my bed until I heard a noise from Charlie's condo this morning. When she woke to get ready for work, I gave up on sleep and lumbered into my kitchen to start some coffee and pathetically wait to see if I could glimpse her when she walked to her car. But when I look outside, I see it snowed, and the cars are covered in white.

Tugging on my clothes from last night and a pair of boots, I can't believe what I'm doing as I do it.

I rush outside and have her car cleaned off before she emerges and sees me. By the time she spots her clean car and turns to smile toward my condo, I'm safely—okay, acting like a pussy—behind my curtains.

I don't know what's gotten into me over this girl. I've never let a woman affect my work, not in this field, anyway. Sure, I've fucked a bunch of them in my financial job, but that was different. People don't die in that line of work by being distracted by pussy.

Which makes me hard again because all I can think about is Charlie's pretty little cunt. Fuck, she was so perfect. Pink and waxed smooth, her tiny little clit peaking out, seeking the attention of my tongue. And she tasted better than sugar on it when she came.

Jesus, I can still smell her on my face, my fingers too, and it's driving me insane because I don't want to wash her scent from my skin.

As Charlie leaves the condo complex, I swear under my breath and curse my luck. The first time in my life a woman gets to me like this, she'd have to be off-limits, goddamn it.

But was she?

Callan's call last night has me confused and plotting my day over my first mug of coffee.

When I spoke with Mac, he was convinced she was working with one cartel to move drugs in and out of the country. It hadn't sat right with me then, but I got distracted by her pictures and went off to beat town with my cock, then forgot all about my questions.

Like why would a cartel from their part of the world run drugs in Lime Peak, Maine? How in the hell did she come into contact with drug runners? I'm guessing it wasn't at a professional conference for teachers of kids with special needs.

Callan's call last night was weird, even for him. The man is quirky, anal retentive, and obsessive-compulsive. All traits that have me again wondering why Mac didn't just have him type some code or shit into a database system and find out if she was in fact tied to the cartel or if something else was at play here.

I open my laptop and find a browser to get the info for the Lime Peak PD. In my experience, there's always an incompetent, overeager cop in a small town like this one who will be all too happy to answer a few questions if I stroke his ego just right. A few clicks through their website and I find pay dirt.

Sergeant Daniel Buzzle.

A little deep diving—I might not be as skilled as Callan, but I can hold my own—turns up he was born and raised in Lime Peak. Single and still living with his mother, his father left them when Dan was not much more than a baby.

I finish my coffee and while a second is brewing, I jump into the shower and ignore the ache in my cock. I'm dressed and pouring the dark brew into my favorite travel mug when a text from my little brother brings a smile to my face.

Rhodes is twenty years younger than Corey and me, a surprise baby who is now in Louisiana studying at Tulane. He has it bad for his best friend's little sister, who is a freshman on campus, and I laugh when I imagine Corey responding the same as me.

Rhodes always gets pissed at our twin connection that over the years, Corey and I started texting the other so our responses would match just to fuck with him. The dude gets so into his own shit, he doesn't stop long enough to think that's what we're doing.

Rhodes: WTF am I going to do about Lake, man? I can't even be in the same room as her w/o springing wood. Forrest is going to fucking kill me.

I send Corey a text to see if he got a similar one, which he did, then we laugh over the fact Rhodes could save himself a lot of energy if he group texted us. But because he's our baby brother, we don't mention that. Instead, we let him torture himself.

I respond to Rhodes with the same answer as Corey, then ignore the rest of his incoming messages until the final one.

Rhodes: I hate you both.
Storm: Love you, little bro.

In my car, I cue up the directions to the station and head out. Turning only a few times, I pass Camp SubLime and the pull toward Charlie is real, and I have to fight the urge to pull into the lot, rush the building, and ask her for a redo.

Arriving at the police station, I find it's Sergeant Buzzle's day off, so I choose to not say too much about who I am or why I'm there. I'm sure I'll get more out of Buzzle than I would any of the cops at the station today. With nothing else to do, I run a few errands, then return to the condo, where I change into my running gear and hit the trails.

As I run over the snow and ice, I can't get Charlie out of my head. Her scent fills my brain and makes running a challenge as my cock inflates over the memory of her in my arms last night, the way she submitted and came for me...multiple times.

When I arrive back at my place, I almost collide with Charlie for a second time in just as many days.

She must have left school early because it's only mid-afternoon when she quickly opens her car door as I'm passing by. If it weren't for my quick reflexes, I would have taken a hit from the door to my body. Instead, I grab Charlie and use my body to catch the brunt of our fall.

She lands directly on top of me, and that annoying erection from the trail springs to life again. I shift her to my hip as not to scare her off, then run my hands over her body to check for any impact injuries.

"Storm." She's breathless. I don't know if it's from the fall, the scare because I surprised her, or if she's as aroused by me as I am by her, but I can't seem to muster up a fuck to give. Charlie is breathless, and I'll take her that way for any reason I can get.

"I'm sorry." I blurt the apology and make it worse when I push my luck. "And for making you come and leaving all within the same five minutes."

"Oh, I...Yeah, that wasn't nice."

I smile up at her. "I know. Let me make it up to you. I went food shopping. I'll cook for you tonight, and I promise it's a meal we *will* eat."

"Didn't like what you had last night?" she asks, and my cock twitches.

I don't care if she feels it now. Not after that sassy response.

I yank her hips and align them back with mine, then grind into her. "You feel how hard you make my cock? I've been like this for hours. I spent the day with the scent of your pussy on my fingers and face. I lost count how many times I brought my fingers to my nose just to smell you again."

"Jesus."

"Say you'll give me another chance, and I promise no running."

I don't know how I managed to talk her into giving me a break, but she agrees to come over in a few hours and let me cook her dinner.

I call my sister-in-law in full panic mode because not only do I not know how to cook a blessed thing, but I'm also uncertain I even have the right supplies.

"Storm?" Lainey asks as her way of answering, confused that I'm calling after just telling her and Corey I was leaving for a mission.

"Yeah. Hey, Lainey. Listen, I need your help with something, but I don't want Corey or Rhodes to hear about this. Probably not Liam either. He's turning into a little shit like his father."

Lainey laughs. "You're okay, though?"

"Yeah, I'm in Maine. Nothing to worry about."

"I won't ask. I know you can't tell me anything, anyway. What do you need my help with? And I'll keep this between us."

I exhale a deep sigh. "I met a girl."

"Don't sound so thrilled." Lainey chuckles.

"No. It's not that. It's that I fucked it up already."

"Wait, are you in Maine for this girl or you literally met her yesterday and already fucked it up?"

"Sort of both, but mainly the last part." I let out another sigh.

"Okay. Take a minute to think about how bad it really is, then tell me what you did."

I do as she says. Lainey is always more level-headed than me. I admit to some of what happened last night, but not everything. My sister-in-law doesn't need the gritty details. "I met this woman who I know some things about, but she doesn't know that or me. I banged into her while on a run and took care of her injuries, so she asked me to dinner. She lives in the place next to where I'm currently staying. We fooled around instead of eating, and I left when I came to my senses over how wrong it was."

Lainey laughs. "That's some story. I'm surprised you're not behind bars. I mean, strange men banging into women while running and knocking them to the ground usually ends with fingerprinting."

"I told her I wasn't a rapist."

Lainey laughs again, this time at my expense. "The fact that you're worse with words than Corey really says something. But back to the way the night ended. You left after you slept with her? Was this abruptly and without an excuse? And please, Storm, I'm begging you, tell me you aren't that much of a dick that last night ended in a happy way for you, but not her, if you know what I mean."

"Oh!" I say when I catch on to what she means. "No, I didn't...ah, I didn't finish, but I made her...I took care of her twice."

Lainey whistles. "Good boy. Okay, so she can't hate you too much."

"She agreed to let me cook for her tonight."

"Ah," Laine says. "Hence the call for help to your favorite sister-in-law."

"Only."

"Don't push your luck. What do you need me to teach you to cook in under two hours?"

"Sauce for pasta? I think I can handle a salad and heating up bread."

Lainey walks me through making what she calls a quick sauce. Luckily, I bought almost everything I needed and the few things I didn't she said won't ruin the meal. I don't admit that I had some help from a woman at the store who led me in the direction of the pasta aisle and told me which ingredients to buy.

Laine and I hang up once I'm sure the sauce isn't going to poison Charlie and I've promised her the rest of the story soon.

I'm running my hands through my hair as I hear Charlie's soft knock on my door.

"Hey," I say when I crack the door open. "Come in."

"Thanks. Um, I brought dessert. Hope you like Whoopie Pies. There's this place in Falls Village called Baker's Kitchen and the owner makes the best varieties."

Charlie places the pastries down as I say, "They sound awesome. Let's make a promise to eat tonight, okay? I want to apologize for the way I behaved last night. I never should have—"

Charlie cuts me off when she leaps into my arms and covers my mouth with hers.

I fall into the kiss, my hands palming her ass and helping her rub against my hard cock. I'm just about to warn she needs to stop or I'm going to embarrass myself when the timer goes off, and she yelps.

We both take a second to catch our breaths after I put her on her feet.

This thing between us has a mind of its own and feels bigger than both of us.

"I'm sorry," she says. "After last night, and now this, you must think I'm either hard up, a slut, or both."

I raise an eyebrow. "Last night, you mentioned it's been a long time since you last had sex."

Charlie laughs and I use the minute to take the bread warming in the oven out and put it on a platter.

"Come on," I offer. "Let's eat and talk. I think we need to figure out this crazy thing going on between us."

"It is nuts, right?" she asks. "I was worried it was only me feeling it."

I grasp my cock through my jeans and look down at my hand. "Not just you. Not even close."

I bring the rest of the food to the table, then tug out a chair for Charlie. When she sits, I do as well, but I pull her chair closer to mine so I can touch her while we eat.

"Go 'head," I encourage. "Help yourself."

I smile inwardly when Charlie takes a second scoop of the pasta and adds a huge hunk of the bread to her plate, saying, "It smells so good. You enjoy cooking?"

"Nah. I had some help in the store picking the ingredients and I called my sister-in-law to walk me through cooking. It was actually pretty simple."

"Well, it looks and smells great."

Charlie moans through her first bite, then lifts a hand, holding me off while she takes another.

I place the warmth of my palm on her thigh to gain her attention and wait for her eyes to find mine. "I love when you moan. Jesus, Char, I need to hear you doing that with my dick in your mouth."

She blushes.

"I'm sorry...again. Let's eat up, then we can see where this goes. I need to apologize again about leaving the way I did last night. It was nothing you did wrong or you in any way."

"The 'it's not me, it's you line'? Storm, please."

"No," I say, lifting her into my lap. "I mean it. I...shit! I don't know how to explain it because there are things I can't tell you."

"Okay." She turns in my lap to straddle me. "So tell me what you can say."

"That was a friend of mine that called last night. I knew what he was calling to say, I probably wasn't going to like. It was something that needed to be private."

"Alright. So you left. At the end of the day, Storm, honestly, you should be mad at yourself, not me mad at you. You took care of me...twice then left with—" She shifts around over my shaft to bring her point home.

"Yeah. That part definitely pissed me off."

Charlie giggles. "Can I ask you something? I guess a few things, actually."

"Sure. But maybe we can go sit on the couch."

I carry her like I did at the trail and plop her on my sofa, then sit next to her. "I can make coffee or tea, whichever you drink. I bought both today."

"Um, I'm good. First question relates to that though. Where are you from and how long are you going to be here?"

"New York, and I don't know."

"Hmm. Do you enjoy my company, or is this just a sexual attraction thing for you?"

"I'm fixated on everything about you. I want to know everything there is to discover and god, do I also want inside that tight pussy, Charlie."

"Okay, how about this...we agree we're sexually attracted to each other and want to have sex? We're both consenting adults. How old are you?"

"Forty-two, you?"

"Twenty-eight. Are you married or with someone special?"

"No." It comes out in an exasperated manner. But then I think about Corey and the debacle between him and Laine and those few years when they were apart. His relationship with another woman was stupid, but it didn't make him a bad person or cause him to love Delaney any less. I clear my throat. "I've never been. With someone, I mean. Not in a committed relationship."

"Oh, one of those, huh?"

I return the smile she sends me. "Yeah, one of those."

"Can I tell you what I want and then you can accept my offer or decline?"

I nod.

"I have a lot of stress at work and that makes finding time for dating challenging. This freakishly small town also doesn't offer many options. The other thing is," she clears her throat and shifts around on the sofa. "I'm in a position of power all day. Even at night and the weekends if I'm out and about. I can never not be in charge when families or the students see me. It's exhausting."

"I know what you need, Char. You need to get out of your head and hand over control so you can find relaxation and peace. I watched you find it last night when you came apart for me. You might not realize this, but the way you submitted to me so quickly says something."

"Yeah, that I'm desperate."

"No." I correct. "That you need a man who can take care of you in bed, and I think I proved that's a role I'm more than qualified to handle."

She stands from the couch and extends a hand to me. "Come on, then. Auditions start in five."

Charlie

I can't believe this is me right now. Accepting this man's weak apology for leaving me questioning what I did wrong last night, admitting I want him to control things in bed, and offering myself to the wolf.

But here I am.

I lead Storm to his bedroom. His condo is laid out the same as mine, so there's no guessing where to go.

He steps into the room behind me and closes the door with a click. "For my *audition*," he says the word with sarcasm, "we'll use the stoplight color system. Green, if you're good and want me to continue. You'll say yellow if you need a break or need things to slow down. If I hurt you or you get scared, red. Understand?"

I nod, but his finger lifting my chin brings our eyes together.

"Rule number one with us," he says. "You use your words like a big girl."

"Yes, Daddy."

He growls from deep down low in his belly. "There's a ton of potential there, sweetheart, but we'll get to that later." He spins me around, then presses his front to my back while my front meets the wall beside his bedroom door.

I moan when I feel his hands meet my shoulders and his lips find my ear. "Shh. Let's start with getting you nice and relaxed, shall we? You're too tense for my liking."

I'm high-strung by nature, but being around him makes my muscles clench even more.

Storm wraps my hair into a bunch and pushes it over a shoulder to expose the sensitive column of my neck where he trails kisses up and down before landing on the spot behind my ear.

His large thumbs press into the nape of my neck the way I love. It's my favorite part of my weekly manicure. There's this one girl who does my neck to perfection. But right now, Storm is giving her a run for her money with the way the wide pads of his thumbs are working the knots away.

I can't control the whimper that escapes as my head lolls back and finds his broad chest. "Holy, god!"

He presses into me, scrapping his teeth all the way to my lobe. He pulls it into his mouth and tugs. "That's a good girl."

His hands on my hips help me grind into him while he grunts through a few thrusts until his hands disappear to find the hem of my shirt. He tugs, then waits. When I don't answer, Storm asks, "You okay with me getting this out of my way?"

"Yes."

He pulls my shirt over my head and instantly frees my breasts from the confines of my bra.

When his fingers pluck at my nipples, he whispers into my ear, "Good remembering to use your words. Keep being a good girl like that for me, and I'll give you a reward."

Goose bumps cover my skin, brought out by the exposure to the air, but more by his words.

I want to be *his* good girl. I want to make him happy. I want him to think I'm doing a good job and give me a reward. I want his praise.

Storm brings us together, chest to chest, then lowers his head to drag my nipple into his mouth.

The bud hardens in a flash of pain and pleasure so seamlessly merged, I'm not sure where one begins and the other ends. It causes my breath to hitch when he pulls back and lets my nipple snap out of his mouth.

"Storm," I plead.

"What, Spunky? Tell me what you need."

"I want to kiss you."

I wait for his lips to cover mine. When they do, I moan into the kiss and lift to my tiptoes.

"You're a tiny little thing, aren't you?"

"Not really. I'm short, but I have never been tiny."

"Honey, I outweigh you by at least a hundred pounds. Trust me, you're tiny."

"You make me feel small in a good way."

Storm smiles. "Good. Is that something you need? Hmm, to feel small and feminine?"

"Yes. At work, I check some days just to be sure I haven't grown a dick."

Storm flings his head back and roars in laughter. "I've had my hand down those pants, Charlie, and trust me, that pussy is fucking perfection."

He tugs my pants down without warning or asking for permission, but leaves my panties in place. "This good?" He checks in.

"Yes, I don't want you to stop doing any of the things you're doing."

Storm smirks. "Wishing I had a few more hands to get on this body?"

I check his eyes to be sure this isn't going where I fear.

"I see that look and no, I don't like to share. These two hands will have to cut it for you, sweetheart."

"All good for me. Two is enough."

He returns to kneading the muscles in my neck and shoulders with his thumbs and hands, his hard length pushing into my belly as he tugs me closer so he can reach every spot on my back.

"How about that?" he asks as he grinds into me. "That enough for you?"

"I'm afraid it's going to be too much."

"You'll take it like a good girl and ask for more when we're done."

"Yes." I sigh. "Yes, Storm. Yes!"

He kisses my neck, my earlobe, then the special space where my neck and shoulder meet. He lingers there for a second, then bites just hard enough to draw a strangled sound from me. "I'm going to take your panties off now, okay?"

"Yes, please."

With my sex exposed, I shiver, but Storm is right there, covering my mound with his warm palm, his thick finger splitting my seam and rubbing in the most perfect rhythm.

He strokes and pets, making me hot for more and on edge for the climax I already feel bubbling in my toes. Then his thumb finds my clit and rubs in a side-to-side motion that's going to make me fly over the cliff into bliss before I can brace myself.

"Storm, I'm going to—"

"Ask me," he demands and eases the pressure. "Ask me to allow you to come. Beg to come for me, Charlie."

"Fuck!" I cry as Storm strokes through my wet folds again. "Please. Storm, please let me come for you. Make me come for you."

He leans in and whispers, his finger all but still now, "Daddy. Make me come for you, *Daddy*. Say it."

"Make me come for you, Daddy."

"Good girl."

Storm circles my clit this time with the right amount of pressure to make me scream his name again. "Storm. Close. Please."

"That's it. Let me give you what you need. You're so beautiful when you're like this, relaxing and giving it all over to me."

I shamelessly spread my legs wider to give him better access to my wetness, and he takes even more than I give, using his foot to kick my legs even wider.

Storm adds a second hand and pumps at least two fingers into me. I feel so full, it could be three. It's tight and wet and I can't help but love the sound of his fingers coated in my arousal, filling the air.

"Come for me," he demands and presses down on my clit, then shakes his thumb, making the vibrations ruin me.

My body trembles and shudders as I come into his hand with his name on my lips.

Storm covers my lips with his to catch my cries. His tongue licks mine along with my lips as his fingers stroke me through my climax.

Trembling in his arms, I thank him for the orgasm, for taking my weight against his body so I don't fall, for making me feel so good I don't ever want this to end.

"My turn now, sweet thing. I need you on your knees begging for my dick."

I'd like to say it's a shock when I drop to my knees and reach for his belt, but it's really not. The way he makes me feel when his hands cup my face and he leans down to take my lips one last time before I take his cock into my mouth, has my heart fluttering and my stomach doing a flip.

"Take it out, baby," he orders. "Lick me, toy with it for a minute, then I want my cock down your throat."

Storm's hands find the wall and he braces himself when the heat of my hand circles his shaft. He's hot and thick, and I stroke his silky flesh in my grasp a few times. Then I tug his pants to his ankles and place my hands on his thighs.

Leaning in close, I open my mouth, but he pulls back and reminds me to ask like a good girl. "Beg me if you want this," he says, while holding his erection out to me.

"Please. I want to suck you. I want to taste you, Storm. I want to make you come in my mouth."

"Jesus, where have you been my whole life?" He lets one hand leave the wall to shove it into my hair. "Open wide and do as I say. Get me nice and wet, then you're going to lick me."

One thrust and his dick taps the back of my throat.

I panic for a second because he's bigger than any man I've ever had like this. No. I've never had a man remotely like this.

My eyes instantly water, and I gag when I feel the tip of his shaft rub my throat.

"Mmm." He hums. "Good girl. I'm nice and wet now. Lick me from root to tip. Show me how much you want my cock."

I lick him like a popsicle, up one side and down the other, swirling my tongue around the ridge just below the head of his cock on each pass. When I flick at his underside, he emits a feral growl and surges his hips forward.

"Okay, enough playing. I want you to suck me now until I tell you to stop. Don't be scared. If it's too much, tap my leg and I'll pull back."

I nod.

One hand cups his sac while I leave the other on his thigh, in case I need an escape route.

Storm groans at my touch, then chuckles. "So naughty. You're going to pay for that later."

I smile around him, then bob my head and force my throat to relax so I can take him as far down as he wants.

Up and down, my mouth works his cock as Storm moans and grunts through each stroke. As he flies closer to the finish line, his words turn dirty, and it's embarrassing how wet and achy they make me.

"Yes, fuck! Suck it, take my cock. Choke on it. So good. Don't stop. Deeper. Want to fuck your tight cunt next. Make you come all over me. Yes. Yes. Fuuuck. More."

Tears cover my cheeks, and I can feel saliva on my chin. The urge to swipe it away almost makes me take my hand off his length where it is now frantically tugging him in time with my mouth. I'm sure I'm a mess, but when I catch his eyes on me and he mouths two words—so beautiful—I focus all my attention on him.

"You're going to make me come," he warns. "I want you to swallow this time. Maybe later, I'll come all over your face. Mark you, Charlie."

I nod because as ridiculous as that seems for a woman like myself, that's exactly what I want. I want to be his.

"Don't stop," he demands. "Don't you dare fucking stop. Swallow. Suck my cock deeper. Shit. Fuck! Here it comes."

As he empties himself down my throat, Storm slips his hands around my throat and gently squeezes until his orgasm subsides.

Once he's spent, he hefts me to my feet and says, "Swallow again."

I do and he watches my throat work whatever was left of his release down.

His thumb wipes my lips, then he shoves it into my mouth for me to suck. When I do, his flaccid cock twitches against my leg as his hands cup my face and he covers my mouth with his.

He growls when he tastes himself there, then pulls back and plants a gentle kiss to my forehead. "Was that the first time anyone ever held your throat like that?"

I nod, then remember his rule. "Yes."

"Good girl. Were you scared?"

"No. I knew I could tap your leg. I knew you'd stop."

"You're amazing, Charlie. Fucking amazing. You did well. Let me get you something to drink, then we can talk about what you liked and what else you want to try."

And I want to do that so badly. I want him to hold me in his arms and call me a good girl again, tell me I'm his, and he wants to show me all the dirty things I've never felt right about asking a man to engage in with me. I want all those things and so much more, but instead of that, I'm forced to answer my phone.

When Storm returns to his room with drinks and dessert for us, he finds me dressed and ready to leave.

"Oh, hell, no!" he roars.

Storm

I see red when I find Charlie dressed and ready to sneak out of my bedroom without explanation or the attention she needs and deserves after what we just did.

I know it's what she needs, even if she doesn't. But I'm assuming she's new to submissive sex, and even though she's falling into the role like a pro, that doesn't mean she doesn't need aftercare.

"I wasn't sneaking out," she claims. "I was going to tell you. I have to go. Something happened at the camp and I—"

I take her into my arms and cradle her face in my hands. Forcing her to look at me, I say, "It's late. It's freezing out there and not safe for you to go anywhere alone. I'll take you."

"What? No. I can—"

"Charlie, this isn't up for debate. I'm driving you to wherever you need to go, then we'll come back here and maybe finally have the chance to talk about a few things. One of them being what this is between us, because if we are going to do this, shit like you thinking you're going out alone in dark and icy conditions will only earn you time over my knee."

Her eyes meet mine, and I see the arousal that statement causes, but then she pushes it away with a shake of her head and jumps into her tough principal persona.

Fine. If this is what she needs right now, I'll give it to her, but there is no way in hell this woman is going out without me.

"Um, that's something you do?" she asks with curiosity. "I mean, it's understandable after the other things."

"We'll discuss this later when we have time for me to explain better. Where do you need to go now?"

"The camp. I'll explain what I can on the way."

My words coming back at me sting. I don't want her to censor what she tells me, but I also understand the need for her to keep her students' and their families' information private.

"Okay, let's go. We'll take my truck. The weather is calling for a storm. If it hits before we can get back, we'll have better luck in my truck than in your little SUV. Which, by the way, I probably need to start a list of all the things I want to talk about because that unsafe for this climate vehicle is on the top of my list."

She looks at me with her mouth agape.

"Yeah, that alpha-hole bullshit you've probably read about to quench your need for a Dominant male in your life is all real."

"Oh, I—"

I open my front door and hold it for her. "You're a submissive, Charlie. No doubt in my mind on that front. And you're in luck." I lead her to my truck, open the passenger door, and deposit her inside. "I just so happen to be a Dominant."

I close her in and jog around to the driver's side. Climbing in, I don't look her way. I start the engine and turn off the radio when it blares my hard rock station. Pulling out of the complex, I finally turn to catch her eyes.

"Does that surprise you? Any of it? About you or me?"

She doesn't even take a beat to answer. "No, it doesn't. But I guess I have a lot of questions."

"As you should. We'll deal with whatever you're walking into at the camp first, then we'll go back to the condo and talk about us. With the storm they're predicting, we're going to be snowed in tonight, anyway."

She's quiet and contemplative until we pull into the camp's parking lot. "I have a staff that lives here. Our live-in residents are the neediest and most challenging, so they need round-the-clock supervision. The ones in Black Bear and Lynx House are eighteen to twenty-two. We keep the boys and girls that age on separate sides of campus, but sometimes they find a way."

"Is that what happened tonight?"

"Sort of. You'll see."

I guess it was best she didn't try to explain further because I don't know if I would have believed her. The scene before us is like something out of a movie from the 80s about wild frat life complete with a foam-filled fountain.

"Rourke," Charlie calls a man's name as she jumps from my truck, not waiting for me to make my way around to open her door. Another item to add to my list of things we need to talk about. "You should have called me earlier. I could have driven over with you."

The man's eyes scan me from top to bottom, then make another sweep. It's not just the perusal of a friend meeting the new guy for the first time, it's a man who also likes what he sees. "Looks like you made it here just fine. I didn't want to bother you." He extends a hand my way. "Rourke Lopez."

"Storm Roland. New to town. I live next door to Charlie."

"Mmm." He hums. "She mentioned that."

"Rourke," Charlie warns. "Have their parents been called?"

"Emily is in her office taking care of that now. We should probably go inside."

I nod to agree because it's freezing out, and the snow just started to fall. I tug Charlie close to my side for warmth and follow Rourke into the administrative building.

An older woman is at a desk dressed in a nightgown with a winter coat covering her pajamas and her hair wrapped in toilet paper. She smiles when she sees me standing behind Charlie. "Is this the man from the trail?" she asks, and I feel the tension roll off Charlie.

I bring my hands to her shoulders but pull them in closer to her throat to send a message with my firm hold. "Yes, Ma'am," I say, then release Charlie to offer a hand to her secretary. "Storm Roland and that incident on the trail wasn't my finest moment."

"Hot damn, speaking of fine—"

"Neet, why are you here?" Charlie asks with a scowl pointed in Rourke's direction. "The weather is going to get dangerous. You should head home."

"Harold drove me. He's in the john. Don't get me started on how many times that man needs to pee. I just wanted to grab the files for the repairmen before the storm hit."

An older gentleman exits what I assume is the bathroom and smiles at the room. "Oh, lots more of you here," he says, then walks my way. "Harold Jenkins, Neet's husband and fearless chauffeur for the evening."

"Storm Roland, I'm Charlie's new neighbor and her driver tonight. It's going to get pretty bad, sir. You and Mrs. Jenkins should head home."

Neet stands when her husband pulls back her chair and takes her hand to help her up. "Don't need to worry about us. We've seen snow before and we'll see it again, God willing."

"Nice meeting you, son. Neet's been talking nonstop about the boy who Charlie is head over heels for."

"Oh, god!" Charlie groans and I chuckle.

"Glad to hear first impressions aren't used as the basis for judgement around here."

"No," another man who must have entered the office while I was listening to Harold speak, says. "We're basing them on the noises we hear through the walls."

"Jesus! Sally, is Ian drunk?" Charlie asks as the Jenkins leave with a smile and hand raise to everyone.

"He's had a few. You know what the idea of being snowed in does to him, so I may have slipped him something to relax in his wine at dinner and another in his coffee at dessert and possibly one more in his bedtime water before Rourke called." She manages that in one breath before heading my way. "We saw Charlie head to your condo earlier," Sally, the art therapist, says. "I'm giddy she brought you here. We thought we'd never get to meet you."

"You said you thought he was a figment of her imagination," Ian adds.

Sally chuckles, then shushes the man who must be her husband or boyfriend and lives with her in the same complex as Charlie and me. She smiles sadly at Charlie.

I pull Charlie closer to my side and lean in to whisper, "Head over heels, huh? That gives me an idea for later." Then I send my fingers into her hair and tug her body into mine. I lean down and capture her mouth as I whisper into our kiss for her friends to hear, "As long as you're a good girl."

Leaving the room with mouths agape, I watch in awe as Charlie handles the situation at the camp with fairness, grace, and hot as fuck authority.

With the students settled back in their dorms and their parents alerted about their prank, Charlie sends Rourke,

Ian, and Sally home before she grabs a few more files from her office and finally agrees to leave herself.

The driving back to the condo is slow going and she thanks me for taking her, finally admitting her car never would have made the trip back and she would have been stuck spending the night on the couch in her office.

"I thought about that," I admit with a smirk. "The naughty schoolgirl feel is strong in there."

I catch her smiling my way out of the corner of my eye, but she doesn't let on if that's something she's tried before. My guess would be no, but it's definitely something she'd consider by the way she's shifting around in her seat.

She sends Neet a text to be sure she and Harold, who I learn is her second husband, arrived home safely before doing the same with the rest of her friends.

When we finally arrive back at the complex, not a speck of ground is visible, and I take Charlie by the hand. "Your place or mine?"

"Can we go to mine?" she asks. "I probably have more food and if we lose power, I have candles."

I nod because she's right. I don't have much food and unless the last tenant left a candle somewhere, I don't have any of those either. "Sure. I'll head over to my place for whatever I have if we need it in the morning."

Charlie lets us into her unit, then locks the door behind us before switching off a lamp she'd left on in the living room.

Silently, I take her hand and walk to the bedroom. But I don't stop in there. I take her into the adjoining bathroom and sit her on the toilet lid while I start the tub.

"What are you doing? It's the middle of the night."

"You're a bundle of stress again. I'm running you a bath where you're going to soak and relax while we talk."

She tries to give me a little huff, but when I ask for bubble solution, she points me in the right direction. "And where would I find those candles you mentioned?"

Charlie points to the linen cabinet.

Once I have the room situated, I approach her and bring her to her feet. "I'm going to take your clothes off, okay?"

"Yes." It's a breathy word that goes straight to my cock.

"First question. When you answer me, do you have the urge to follow it up with anything?"

Her eyes look up into mine as I lift her shirt over her head and unhook her bra. "Like what? What do you mean?"

I give a gentle shrug. "Sir or maybe Daddy?"

"Oh."

I laugh, then cup her breasts in my hands from behind and run my thumbs over her nipples. "The thought of it does this to me." I press my erection into her back. "You feel that?"

"Yes."

"Yes?"

"Yes, Daddy."

"Christ, I hoped that was the one you were going to pick. When you used it last night, I was afraid it was a fluke."

I pull her panties down with her pants and hold her steady while she steps out of them. Falling to my knees in front of her, I plant tiny kisses around her pussy until her fingers go into my hair and her hips rock.

Using my thumbs, I open her folds and give her a lick with my flattened tongue. All the way from her sweet entrance to her throbbing little clit.

I moan as her taste hits my tongue. "You're so sweet. Would it help you relax so we could talk if I made you come like this before?"

"Please. Yes. Oh, fuck! More please, Daddy."

"Good fucking girl," I praise and as a reward for that, I devour her cunt with my mouth.

It doesn't take Charlie more than a few well-placed swipes to come for me, and once she settles, I lift her in my arms and carry her to the tub.

Placing her inside, I turn and remove my shirt, then kill the lights.

I plan to sit on the tile floor when she says, "There's enough room in here for you, too."

Without question, I remove my clothing and climb in behind her. It's a tight fit, and water sloshes out onto the floor, but we can make it work.

I tug her between my legs and shift my cock for comfort, then rest my hands under her breasts. "I don't know how long I'll be here or what I can offer you other than this while I'm here, but I'd like to talk about exploring your sexual needs together."

Her nipples pebble at my touch, and I twist and tug them until her head falls to my shoulder and she squirms. "What does that look like?" she asks through quick breaths.

"We give each other our trust. We communicate openly about our wants and needs, what we like and don't. We're exclusive and behind closed doors, you'll submit to me and do everything I say. If you disobey me, I'll punish you."

"Behind closed doors? But in public?"

"The same rules apply, but we'll engage in the non-mainstream activities more subtly."

"Non-mainstream?" she asks and finds my thighs with her hands.

"Yeah, like calling me Daddy. I get that for some it's off-putting. I wouldn't expect you to call me that in front of your friends."

"In private, you want me to call you that, though?"

I cup water in my hands and pour it over her head, then massage her scalp with my fingers.

Charlie moans and I kiss her temple. "When we scene, yes. That means when we have sex or do anything sexual, you'll address me as such."

I run my hands down to her throat and give her a moment to swallow and get a gulp of air before I squeeze.

"You give me your trust so easily. I've seen women that never get to this point where they allow their partner to do this."

I let go and Charlie takes in a deep breath then rolls in my arms to lay her front on mine.

Our eyes meet and then hers slip to my lips.

"Open communication means you can always ask me for what you want. I see you looking at my lips. Tell me what you need."

"I want you to kiss me."

"Good girl. Don't ever hesitate to ask me for what you need. Even if you've been a bad girl and are being punished, your needs are my priority. I might not give you what you want in that moment, but I will make sure your needs get met, always."

I bring her face to mine in my hands and lick her bottom lip before using my tongue to open her mouth. I sweep in and taste her sweetness, our tongues twining and dancing as her hand snakes between us and she wraps it around my cock.

"Charlie," I warn. "We have other things to talk about, but if you keep doing that, I won't be able to think."

She smiles at me. "I thought you said you'll give me what I want."

"What you need, not want, but..." I groan when her thumb runs over my head and toys with the opening there. "That feels so fucking good. You want my cock, baby?"

"Yes, Daddy. I *need* it."

My cock jumps in her hands.

"Fuck. Tell me. Where? How do you need it?"

She pumps me in her grasp, her hand running from my base to the tip, then back down again. Her thumb circles the ridge under my head, and I lose myself in the glorious sensations for a moment.

"I want to do this. I want to watch your dick come in my hand."

She strokes my hard flesh causing tingles to singe my spine and I know I need to slow her ministrations down or I'll be giving her what she wants long before I should.

I laugh as I cover her hand with mine to ease her grip and slow her strokes. "Well, if you keep that up, it's not going to take long with the way you're looking at my cock like that while jacking me off."

Charlie gets on her knees between my legs so she can wrap both hands around my length and I shiver at the sensations already creeping up my spine and the anticipation of her sucking my cock into her warm, wet mouth.

I look down at her tits hanging in front of my dick, and I pinch her nipples hard.

They're pink and perfectly round, not too big, but not exactly small, either. They pebble around her areola as her tips harden into tight buds, and Charlie flings her head back with a moan.

"Rub the head of my cock on your nipples," I order and groan from the pit of my stomach when she does. "Use them to make those nipples ache until you can't take it anymore."

Charlie Tyler is a stunning woman every second of the day. But on the brink of a climax, she breaks every standard for gorgeous. Her skin flushes pink from the tip-top swells of her tits to the point of her perky little nose. Her lips part in an O and redden while her cheeks tinge as if she's embarrassed by her response to the pleasure she seeks.

My heart expands in my chest as I watch her. The way she looks at me with such trust and honesty has me forgetting all about my throbbing cock and my climax climbing up.

This isn't usually an issue. I can go for hours without worrying about coming before I want, or I can come in a second and get the hell out of a situation I find turning emotional that I want to avoid.

But with Charlie, everything is different.

I don't want to avoid the emotional part of sex. I don't want to rush and force out a climax to escape her. I want to spend every second of every day buried deep inside her, then wake up and do it all over again.

But she's continued to work my cock in her grip while my heart defrosted and opened to the idea of loving her and my head processed the fact that I was completely fucked, and now I was going to come whether or not I liked it.

"Shit. Pull me faster. I'm close. So fucking close. You're going to make me come if you keep jacking me like that. You want to watch it? Come on," I beg. "Jerk that cock off and make me come. Yes, yes, yes. Fucking good girl. Good fucking girl. I'm gonna come on those tits."

Charlie jacks me at warp speed, and I roar as my release fills my balls and they pull up tight to my body.

Flinging my hands into her hair, I hold her in place and thrust, fucking her hands as she strokes me through their tight tunnel.

I explode with a grunt into her hand, covering her tits and neck. A glop meets her lips and another lands in her hair. We both watch as stream after stream of my thick white release coats her, one last spurt landing on a nipple and hanging from it.

When my orgasm subsides, I use my fingers to rub my cum around in her tight buds, then collect a little from the tip before I offer it to her.

Without hesitating, Charlie sucks my finger clean with a sigh, then says, "Thank you, Daddy."

Jesus fucking Christ, I might have just fallen in love with her for more reasons than one.

Charlie

With live-in students, snow doesn't deter us from much, but with most of the academic teaching staff living off campus, a huge storm changes the daily schedule, which is never a good thing at Camp SubLime. But Rourke promised me he had everything under control and talked me into taking the two days off.

Storm and I spent those two days it took for the camp to reopen together. Most of that time was spent in bed, but we never had actual penetrative sex. We talked, we ate junk foods straight from their bags, and he held me in his arms on the sofa for late afternoon naps.

He says making us wait for the sex part until we're both crazy, out of our minds for it, will make it all the better, but I think he's holding back for another reason. I just don't know what that is.

When I tried to probe, Storm warned me against being naughty. He insisted I wasn't ready for a spanking for being a bad girl yet.

I'm not so sure. But I'd like to try.

As I walk into the staff room for lunch, I'm trying to come up with a way to get him to tell me why he's holding back instead of taking me over his knee. That's why I don't see the smirks on my friends' faces at first or hear their topic of conversation.

The first thing I hear is Sally's voice. "'As long as you're a good girl,' he leaned in and whispered as he kissed her right there in the main office in front of all of us."

Emily moves her eyes in my direction, then smirks when they connect. "Substantial research shows couples into BDSM are no more likely than the general population to suffer psychiatric problems, and they have no psychological disorders unique to their kinky proclivities."

"Good to know," I state. "Not sure why that's the topic of this conversation, though."

"'A good girl', Charlie, please. We read Fifty Shades as a group." Emily continues, totally ignoring my discomfort.

I roll my eyes. "What does that have to do with anything?"

"I saw the way he looked at you like you were Little Red, and he was the Big Bad Wolf," Rourke adds. "You know, Brad and I went to a club once on vacation."

"Oh, I remember you telling me about that," Ian adds. "And I agree with you, that guy is definitely into the Fifty Shades stuff."

"How would you know, Ian?" I whisper-yell as not to gain any more attention than we already are. "I mean, do you even remember a thing from the other night after the special drinks Sally made for you?"

Shana high-fives her best friend. "I told you. Works every time."

"Wait," Ian stammers. "That was premeditative drugging? You said you gave me a little too much on accident."

Sally chuckles. "Ian, you're a good man, but when it comes to being snowed in, you're a pussy. There, I said what I said."

"He really is."

"It's all your fault!" Ian bellows at his brother. "You're the one that got us stranded for days."

All eyes go back and forth between the siblings, and I sit back and enjoy the reprieve of attention.

"This is why they're a perfect match," Shana says. "He needs to color more."

"I might need to expand my scope," Emily says in my direction. "I hear you were into it."

"Harold and I used to get kinky back when we first started dating after my first husband passed, God rest his soul."

That has all of us gagging, reaching for our drinks, and holding our stomachs while Neet laughs at our expense.

"But he seemed nice?" Kayley asks. "Charlie deserves a nice guy. Maybe she likes the sexy stuff. Leave her alone. It's been forever since she...you know?"

"Hey! Isn't there some HIPAA law or something?"

"I'm not your doctor, Char."

"Well, see if I tell you anything anymore." I harrumph.

None of us having any food in our apartments after the storm, we were forced to order lunch and without many options, we decided the cafeteria would have to do.

We're quiet as Timmy Brown and Mia, the ringleaders of the vandalism from the other night, appear with our meals.

We run a full kitchen at the camp to help teach the kids employable life skills. We also use it as punishment when you decide to skinny dip in the fountain in the middle of a Maine winter after adding bubble bath and food coloring to the icy water. And if that was all of it, this kitchen duty would be the end of their consequences. Unfortunately, these two abide by the principles of go big or go home. They're just lucky they weren't sent home.

Damn hormonal teens.

Which reminds me of my dilemma.

I know I shouldn't ask this group for help because telling them what I need to, is only going to open the floodgates for ridicule, but they're all I have.

I clear my throat. "So, um...let's just say one was with a man who was into some stuff and refused to have sex until he said she was ready. But she is ready. Like so ready. And she wants to be a bad girl and see what it's like to be spanked over his knee. What...um...what do you think a girl should do to make that happen? I mean hypothetically, of course."

The group smirks and together says, "Of course."

They're little to no help with ideas and do nothing but tease me until the bell rings and we head our separate ways.

The hours drag by as I wait for the end of the day when it's time for me to head home. Storm made me promise we'd have dinner together, and I still haven't come up with a good plan to get what I want as I pull into my parking spot a few cars down from his truck.

On my way into my unit, I'm called away from my plotting when my phone rings.

Sergeant Buzzle.

I answer, confused, because I can't imagine what else we could have to talk about. My identity has been stolen. He gave me all the ways to protect it in the future—even though he said they were all useless—and told me he was filing the paperwork in the crazy event someone commits a terrible crime and uses my name as their alias.

And I did everything he told me to do. I called my bank and put special holds and alerts on my accounts. I did a credit check with all three of the top agencies. Anything that wasn't mine—and there were a bunch—I had canceled.

"Hello?" I ask. "Sergeant Buzzle, how can I help you?"

"Miss Tyler?"

"Yes, it's Charlie."

"Hi, Charlie."

"Um, hey. What's wrong? Did someone use my identity for something else?"

"I'm sure. Did you do everything on those papers I gave you?"

"Yeah."

"Okay, good. Anyway, I'm just calling to let you know, and this could be a coincidence and not related, but a dude came in here asking for me. He mentioned he has some questions about the camp and the owner. I met with him, and he says he's working with a private agency on a case. You know anything about that?"

"No, I...Maybe it's one of the parents. Some of them have more money than good sense, and it wouldn't be the first time one of them hired a PI over some nonsense. This current group of teenagers has been pulling pranks and getting into trouble."

"Yes, Miss Tyler, we're very aware."

I clear my throat. "I know. I'm sorry for all the trouble lately."

"It's what we're here for." He grumbles. "Just keep your eyes open and if anyone bothers you, you let us know."

"Um, okay. Thanks."

"Good night."

Well, that's unsettling, but I'm sure this has something to do with Timmy Brown putting his hands on Mia. Her family was the one I was talking about earlier with more money than good judgement.

I make my way through my apartment and send a quick message to Storm to let him know I'll be over within the hour. I need time to devise a plan.

As I'm wracking my brain for one, I get a text from Rourke.

Rourke: I told Brad about your dilemma. He thinks you should march your fanny over there tonight in nothing but a coat.

We parted ways after lunch, and I may have shared a little more with my closest friend.

I like Storm. I'm not sure where this thing between us is going, if anywhere, but I know one place I want it to go sooner rather than later and that's his bed.

Storm is sexy and this Daddy thing is what every one of my other relationships has been lacking. There's so much more of it I want to explore, but he's cutting me off with sex, and I'm at a loss.

Rourke: He said you should act like a brat, all pouty and foot stompy, then tell him you did a whole bunch of things he won't like. You know, like how you said he grumbled over you opening doors on your own and that alpha-shit.

Hmm. The naked under my coat might work as a turn on, but haven't I already been turning him on? I had his dick down my throat. How much more turned on could I make him?

But I do like the bratty thing. That could work because Storm definitely has that alpha-hole thing down pat.

Charlie: Not half bad.
Rourke: Trust me, it's not. Brad and I may have been inspired.
Charlie: Glad I could help. I'll let you know tomorrow if it works for me.

Needing some motivation, I cue up the standard website for free porn and enter *bratty girl makes her Daddy mad* in the search box.

I don't find exactly what I'm looking for right away. It takes a few videos to find something my style. But I do finally hit the jackpot.

Thirty minutes later, with my coat cinched tight and nothing underneath it, I stroll next door in a pair of boots and ring Storm's bell.

He answers, opening the door and allowing his eyes to freely roam my figure a minute before his brain catches up with his eyes and he realizes what he's looking at.

"What's this?" he asks with his finger reaching out to travel up and down, indicating my body. "And those?"

"Nothing," I state nonchalantly and use my finger to loosen the belt on my coat. "Daddy." Pushing the garment off my shoulders, then twirling my pigtails he asked about, I add, "Nothing at all."

Storm's eyes heat as he reaches to tug me into his unit and out of eyeshot of anyone but him. "What the hell are you doing?"

I stomp my foot like I've witnessed the little ones in the preschool do every day. "Don't you like me naked?"

"I like you naked just fine. What I don't like is you outside for everyone else to see like this. Especially when it's freezing, and you could get sick. Are you being a brat on purpose, Charlie? It seems like you're trying to provoke me."

Storm slams his front door, swings me around, and cages me in. His hands yank on the belt of my coat to tug me tighter into his hard chest.

"Why would I do that?" I ask with a small chuckle, not meeting his eyes. "I'm a good girl, Daddy."

"Hmm, I don't know. Maybe you're trying to get yourself punished and decided being a brat is the way to go with me. Maybe you're horny and instead of asking me to meet your needs with open communication, you've got it into this pretty little head of yours that acting like a brat is how you can get me to fuck you until you can't see straight."

I shrug, then pout my lips.

Storm growls. "Is that what this is about? You watched some crap porn about bratty girls getting their asses lit up and here we are, am I right?"

"Maybe," I say, lifting my chin now in defiance to meet his stare.

"I must have done a real piss-poor job of explaining how this works if you think provoking me into spanking your ass until you can't sit down before fucking you senseless is how it works."

I stomp my foot again. "Okay, fine. I've got some stress I'm not sure what to do with and I'm attracted to you beyond anything I'm used to. This thing going on between us has me constantly thinking about you and sex and...and needing it. Rourke and Brad said this would work."

"Are Rourke and Brad active in Daddy kink?"

"Well, no. But—"

"Charlie, if this is going to work the right way, we need to communicate. Tell me what's going on."

I huff in a breath. "I'm scared."

His eyes widen. "Scared. Of what? Did something happen? Did someone threaten you?"

"No, not exactly."

Storm lifts me into his arms, cradling my body, and marches to the sofa, where he plops himself down with me in his lap. "Talk. Now," he orders and tugs my hair free of the ties holding it back.

I exhale. "I've had my identity stolen. The sergeant in town called me last week and alerted me. I spoke to him again today, and he said someone was at the station asking questions about the camp and me. Now I'm freaking out that the people who have my information are after me."

"Why would they be after you?"

"They know my address and everything about me. They forged IRS checks, and I threw them out. I thought they were a scam. Now, I'm piecing all of it together. So, what if they think I cashed them and I have the money?"

"What the fuck?"

"I know."

"I...Charlie, baby, I know you're scared, and I promise you're safe with me, but I need to take care of something."

"What? Now? Where are you going?"

"I was going to text you, but then you beat me to it, coming over here in nothing but this coat."

"Oh, um...no. It's fine. I can eat something at my place. I'm a big girl."

"Fuck that. No, I'm not saying I'm leaving you. You're coming with me. I'm just saying we need to table this for a minute while I deal with a situation."

"Oh. I guess I can come for a ride. I kind of don't want to be alone. But I need to get some clothes."

Storm pushes his hands through my hair. "This scenario has way too much potential for me to let you do that. You were a bad girl, Charlie, and now you'll have to accept the consequences. I'll heat the car, so you won't be cold, but you'll go as you are."

"Storm, I can't possibly—"

My breath hitches when he juggles me around, and I'm laying on my stomach over his lap. I feel a whoosh of cool air as he lifts my coat to expose my ass, then another when his hand flies through the air.

Slap.

"Oh. Oh, my."

Slap.

"Shh, you're to be quiet when you're being spanked unless I ask you to talk. If you're not, I'll start over every time you make a sound."

Spank. Slap. Slap. Slap.

"Fuck, Charlie, this ass. Four more, bad girl. Get ready, these last ones are going to sting."

Storm leans over and grabs something from the table beside the sofa. I hear his labored breathing, then feel the burning sting.

Crack.

94

"Ow."

"Shh, now that one didn't count."

Crack. Crack. Crack.

"Two more than we're done."

I see the magazine he must have used for those last swats, then I feel his palm again for two more blows to my aching flesh.

Before I know what's happened, Storm has me on my feet and he's pulling down my coat.

"I'm guessing that has your pussy wet and aching. Shame we can't do anything about that for a bit. Let's go. We'll talk about how that made you feel in the truck."

Storm

I knew there was something not right about this case, Mac, and definitely Callan Black. My friends were hiding something from me, but damn if I knew what.

I'm afraid if I tip my hand and show Charlie my cards, she'll lose all trust in me and also hand me my balls on a platter for lying to her. Mac will be a dead end as always. The man was an iron wall. But Callan had a weak spot and conveniently was only a few miles away.

"Where are we going?" Charlie asks as she squirms in her seat.

I turn on the heater to warm her buns with a smile. "Falls Village. Are you sore and uncomfortable or are you in pain?"

"Uncomfortable. But...not just my ass."

I chuckle and shift my throbbing erection. "I bet. We'll take care of that as soon as we get home. Then, if your ass is still sore, I have some cream at my place that'll help. Tell me how you felt when I was spanking you."

"Like a naughty child who did something wrong."

"Did you like the sensations from the spanking?"

She looks at me incredulously. "You heard me mention the uncomfortable situation, no?"

My hand squeezes her knee. "A sassy mouth like that will get you another spanking instead of that orgasm you're jonesing for."

And then she does it. The move of disrespect that's the hot button of most men. It's definitely mine.

Charlie rolls her eyes.

Instead of continuing up the hill to the castle where Callan lives with his wife and family, I pull the truck over and unbuckle. Reaching across the cab, I do the same to Charlie, then say, "On your knees with your face to the window, ass pointing my way."

"What? No! People can see us."

"Should have thought of that before firing off that pretty little mouth, then rolling those insanely beautiful eyes at me. You didn't know that was a big no-no, so this time, you'll only get five. The next time, eye rolling is ten. On your knees."

"Storm, I can't. What if someone sees? I know people here."

"Hmm. The windows are dark enough and it's dark out. I'm not asking you to get out of the car and bend over the hood. Although—"

"No! Okay," she agrees and moves to her knees with a glare over her shoulder at me.

I lift her coat and thank the stars above that she followed through with this crazy idea of hers because the easy access to the parts of her I need is convenient.

I rub my palm over her red globes and feel a pang of guilt that I didn't give her after-care once her first run at a spanking ended, but other issues need to be addressed. Unfortunately, instead of taking care of those now, here I am with her ass in my face, her pussy glistening for me, and my hand itching to teach her a lesson.

"Five," I say. "Count. They'll be fast."

I run my finger over the redness of her cheeks, then let it slip through her wet folds.

"Oh, yes," she moans. "Please do that instead."

Charlie clenches around my finger when I let it slide deep inside her. Curling it to rub her sensitive spot inside, I bring my other hand to her ass.

Slap. Slap. Spank. Spank. Crack.

"Five," she breathlessly states. "I think I'm going to come."

I leave my finger inside her, but I stop all movement. "That wasn't for your pleasure," I state. "You want to fuck my finger and come? You'll accept the consequences of doing so without permission. Or you can stop rocking those hips and wait until we get home, and you earn an orgasm."

She sends me a defiant glance before she throws her head back and cries out as her body shakes from her climax.

I laugh. "You're not going to be able to sit for a month, bad girl."

She's breathless, but she scoffs at me when I pull her coat down, then her eyes glaze over when I pop my wet finger in my mouth and suck it clean.

Pulling up Callan's driveway, I turn to Charlie. "Your pussy is such a fucking aphrodisiac. I can't wait to have you sitting on my face later. Until then, I need to talk to my friend quick. You want to come in or stay here? I won't be long."

"Can I come?"

"Charlie." She turns her head to me. "Good girl. Should have asked that before you came on my finger, but..." I laugh. "Yes, you can come inside with me. Stay in your seat and let me come get you. I don't think your ass can take much more tonight."

I retrieve her from the truck and lead her to the massive entry door.

I pound my fist on the substantial wood.

Black has top security, so I know he's aware I'm here after allowing me through his gate at the bottom of the hill.

"Mr. Roland," Callan says as he opens the door, and his eyes grow wide when he sees Charlie tucked into my side. "And Miss Tyler."

I look between the two. "Do you two know each other?"

"I knew Charlie's father very well."

"Callan is a huge supporter of the camp."

I raise an eyebrow. "Interesting, Black."

He shrugs. "What do you need, Storm?"

"Ah, Charlie is facing a bit of trouble and you came to mind," I say. "Maybe you can help."

"Sure. What's the problem?"

"Are you going to invite us in, or are we going to talk while we freeze on your porch?"

"We'll be quick. You're a big man, don't be a pussy. She's close enough to you for warmth."

I roll my eyes at the man's lack of social skills, but Charlie doesn't miss a beat.

"Callan," she says. "If Jordan knew you had guests, would she like that they were on the porch because you didn't invite them in?"

Callan huffs. "I hate this social shit. Fine, come inside."

I smile at Charlie, and the connection comes together. "Black, how exactly did you meet Charlie's dad?"

"I went to Camp SubLime when I was a kid. He was cool and let me have my space and didn't force all these social niceties down my throat. We stayed in touch. When I had the means, I started supporting the camp."

I feel Charlie's stare as Callan makes eye contact, and we have a wordless conversation about people in the area knowing he, Ace Lyons, and Elliot Montgomery have some military affiliation but because they don't bring harm into Falls Village and its neighboring towns, people pretend the three live a civilian's life.

I get it. I don't say much to even my twin, less to Rhodes and our parents. It's not an easy life.

"Charlie," I say with a hand going to her back. "I think Mr. Black and I need a minute. Let's get you back into the truck and we'll talk on the porch where you can see us."

Charlie's eyes lock with mine, and I give her a stern eyebrow lift that says it's not up for discussion.

She stomps a foot to which Callan chuckles and mumbles something about me having a live wire on my hands. Damn straight.

I lead her to the truck, seat her inside, then turn the engine and seat warmers on. "I'll only be a minute, and I already know you're pissed. We'll talk it through when I'm done." With that, I slam the door shut and make my way back to Callan's porch, where he's waiting for me.

"You knew her when you looked into her for Mac. What the hell, Black? Something about this case hasn't sat right with me from the start. If you knew her father, and Mac thought she was knee deep in drug shit, I can't imagine you'd let him send me out here."

"Mac knows my connection. Too close to home. I did the background intel, then he removed me from the case and switched out to you."

"She's not smuggling drugs! She's had her identity stolen. I also find it hard to believe you didn't know that."

Black shrugs. "Maybe I'm off my game. I've been out for years, only getting a bone here and there when Mac needs me."

I roll my eyes and remember what I told Charlie about that habit earlier. "That's some kind of bullshit, and you know it. If she's in danger..." I get in his face. "And I find out you didn't tell me."

Callan shoves me back. "You know how I feel about personal space, man. Back up. And I wouldn't put Charlene in danger. The identity theft thing is unrelated. I'll look deeper into it if it'll make you feel better."

"Why the hell am I here, Black?"

Callan shrugs again. "Question for the boss."

As Callan extends a hand, I growl. I know that isn't easy for him, so I take it with a slow smile.

"I might be shit with social cues, but I know a man with a hard-on over a girl and you've got one for her. Mac won't be thrilled about that."

"Yeah, well, I'm not thrilled about whatever game he's playing. If she's in danger, I need to be made aware."

Callan nods. "I'll see what I can do. Give it until morning. Call me before you reach out to Mac."

I nod in thanks, then jog back to my car as an unexpected snow begins to fall.

When I get into the truck, Charlie is wringing her hands.

"What's wrong?"

"I just got an alert on my phone. We're getting hit with a huge, unexpected storm that was supposed to go off to sea. It shifted, and we're going to get hammered. Luckily, most of the extra staff arrived last night and the kids on break aren't expected for a few days, but I should make sure everything is covered at the camp.

"Call Rourke. Tell him we're out and can swing by. No reason for him to go out too."

With that settled, I turn the truck in the camp's direction.

"Why don't you just drop me off?" Charlie says. "I can't leave them without someone in charge, so I should stay. I'll be fine. You can still make it home."

I laugh. "Not happening. I'm staying."

"Storm, you don't need to do that. I'm going to be stuck either in my office or a dorm room. You'll be miserable. The kids aren't easy to be around for days in tight quarters, either."

I put the truck in park and shoot her a glare to stay put until I open her door. Opening it, I say, "I'll be miserable without you. I'm staying. And I have a niece and a nephew. They think I'm cool. Kids love me. Plus, staying in your office might be fun. How do you feel about being spanked on your desk?" The arousal hits behind her eyes and I smile. "Good. It's settled. Let's go."

Entering the administrative building, Charlie heads right for her closet, then sends me a sad smile. "I need to put clothes on, obviously. I keep some here in the event I'm puked or peed on."

I approach her and take her into my arms, pulling her tightly to my chest. "That's fine for now. But once you're done with everything you need to do, Mr. Roland needs to see you in his office." I rub my hands together. "You were naughty, Miss Tyler and the Headmaster needs to address and correct your behavior."

"Corporal punishments aren't allowed at my camp, Mr. Roland."

"It's all good. In this scenario, it's my school and you're the misbehaving student."

Charlie sucks in a deep breath right before our lips meet for a heated kiss.

Pressing my erection into her stomach, I groan. "Now, get to work, so we can play. This office turns me the fuck on."

Charlie goes for her desk and fires up her desktop to email the staff, so they'll know she's on the campus if needed. She checks back in with Rourke, who promises to relieve her as soon as he can, but once she tells him I'm with her, he rests easy and says they'll stay in touch.

She calls the maintenance crew to be sure the generators are going to click on if we lose power and tells them to be ready to remove the snow as soon as it stops falling.

I watch her with awe as she commands respect and gets it without question. She's in charge, organized, and level-headed in a time of need.

"Wow," I say, coming up to massage her shoulders from behind her office chair. "Watching you rule this empire of yours has my dick hard as fuck."

She giggles. "I thought I was in trouble?"

"Oh, you are. I'm not forgetting about any of that, trust me," I say, adjusting my erection, then stroking myself over my pants. "I'm ready to play when you are."

"I need to do a walkthrough of the campus and make sure everyone is where they belong. You can stay—"

I tip her chair back, so our eyes meet, and she squeals.

"You're not leaving my sight."

"Oh. Did Callan say something about the identity thing? Are they looking for me?"

I frown. "What? No. I told you, you're safe with me."

"Because you know Callan, which means whatever it is he and his friends really do for a living, so do you. Did someone send you here to protect me?"

I clear my throat. "No."

"Then why are you here?"

"I can't—"

"I know. You can't tell me. Okay. I guess I'm going to have to trust you then."

A tight ball forms in the pit of my stomach because I want that trust so badly, but I know when I tell her the truth, that trust I've earned is going down the drain.

I follow Charlie in and out of the dorms, each housing different aged students. The youngest are adorable and get super excited to see her. Some ask questions about my presence, while others don't even seem to notice me.

We hold hands as we march through the snow to the other side of campus, and I stop her under the moonlight and take her into my arms. "Charlie, I feel like shit I can't tell you some stuff, but I want you to know this was completely unexpected. I never thought I was coming to Maine and going to find...you. This. I'm not typically a romance or relationship guy, but with you, all that changed, and I want to kiss you while this snow falls around us so fucking badly. So bad."

Our lips meet in a gentle sweep and we both moan into the embrace.

I lick at her lips when her hands come to my chest. "I love the feel of your touch on me. You're so perfect."

She pulls back and studies me for a moment, then lets her eyes slide shut when I part her lips with my tongue and sweep inside to taste her.

"There's a lot I like about you, too," she says, pulling away and taking me toward another dorm. "And you were just as unexpected."

As I hold the door open for her, she warns me it's the housing for the oldest boys who are the most challenging. "They have big mouths, and they like to think they have the balls to match, but inside, they're really scared children who have next to no control over their emotions. Ignore anything they say. One of them has coined a nickname for me that's inappropriate at best. He's been punished repeatedly for it, but with you here, I can almost guarantee he's going to show off."

"I'll let you handle it. I think watching you in professional mode will be good foreplay for what I have in mind when we get back to your office."

I watch the change in her demeanor when a handsome boy, who by the looks of him is about the same age as my nephew, smirks in her direction.

"Here we go," she says. "That's Nicky."

"Is he allowed to be in nothing but skivvies?"

"In his room, but he's been working out and has developed a love for his body right along with the girls on campus he's all over."

I groan. "I remember being this poor kid's age. All I thought about was getting pussy or my dick sucked."

"Please don't tell him that," she begs, then turns to the boy. "Mr. Gillespie, before you say anything, let me remind you that you're still working off your last remark. This is Mr. Roland. Say hello, then it's lights out in ten minutes. I'm here for the evening because of the storm. Your house principal should have told you all about the unexpected weather."

A smirk covers his face. "Yes, Ms. Tyler. I was just getting ready for bed when I heard you were coming by for a visit with a..." His eyes scan over me. "Friend. Lucky man." He extends a hand to me.

I shake it, then release my firm grip.

"That's enough, Nicky. Don't get yourself into any more trouble this week."

He lifts a chin, says good night, and closes his door.

"Wow!" Charlie says as we make our way out of the dorm. "He's either enamored by you or scared to death."

I let out a huge bellow. "I'm guessing scared to death. I didn't get the gay vibe."

"No. He's been experimenting too much with the girls for me to suspect that, honestly. But he's usually sassier with me. The nickname—"

"What does he call you?"

"CT."

"Your initials?"

"Hmm. Mmm." I hum.

"What? What's so bad about that?"

"He plays it off that he calls me that for my initials, but that's not why. One of the five-year-olds went home for a long weekend to his parents. The dad is an asshole at best who is mentally abusive to the kid and physically abusive to the mom. When the kid tells us stuff, we're mandated reporters, so we have to file a report each time he says anything we deem unsafe. I call on this kid's dad a lot. He told the boy to stop telling me stuff and apparently referred to me as a fucking cunt. The kid, not knowing what he was saying, called me that in front of some of the older boys. Word got out and CT was born. Nicky enjoys pushing the envelope."

I cover the chuckle with the back of my hand.

"What?" she hits me in the chest. "It's not funny."

"It's hysterical. First, if a five-year-old said that in my presence, I would be on the floor rolling like a child. Second, if I were fourteen, and I heard a little kid say that to a teacher, I would have come up with that nickname, too. Sorry. Not saying it's right, and he deserves to be called to task, but just saying it's to be expected."

She growls as we make our way back into the building where her office is. "Let me do a few more things. Then we can figure out where we're going to sleep for the night."

"Not so fast, Miss Tyler. I believe you were sent to see me about your behavior," I say, getting into character and smirking when I watch Charlie change into the naughty schoolgirl I know she wants to be punished for.

Charlie

"You can call me sir in this scene," Storm says as he gets comfortable in my chair. "Now, tell me what you did, little girl."

My insides go to mush and a finger makes its way into my mouth, causing Storm to groan and shift in my seat.

"Miss Tyler, come here."

I slowly walk over to where Storm is sitting in my chair, then stop at the side of my desk. "Yes, sir?"

"Good. Now, your teacher told me you showed up to class in nothing but a coat? Is that right?"

"Sir, I—"

Storm holds up a silencing hand, and I smirk because the number of times I've tried that in real life with no success was embarrassing. But it works for him, and I zip my lips.

"I need to see this coat. Go put it on the same way you went into class."

I nod, grab my coat off the chair, and head into my bathroom. When I return, Storm has turned off the industrial overhead lighting, switching it out for the lamp I keep on the end table near my loveseat.

Storm's eyes lift when he sees me in my coat, knowing there is nothing underneath. He stands and reaches his index finger in my direction, calling me forward.

When I'm close enough for him to reach, he wraps his fingers into the belt loops and uses them to pull me flush to the front of his body.

Feeling his hard length against me, I moan. "Sir, I'm sorry for being a bad girl. I won't do it again. I promise."

"I'm very disappointed in you, Miss Tyler. And being sorry isn't enough for you to learn your lesson. I'm afraid I'm going to have to punish you."

I glance at his feet, unable to meet his eyes even though this is a game, and I haven't actually done anything wrong. The thought of disappointing him turns my stomach, and I don't want him to see that anguish in my eyes.

His finger lifts my chin. "Are you afraid it's going to hurt?"

I shake my head.

"Are you lying to me? Because that's only going to make this harder on you, not me, Spunky."

As my eyes are forced to his, they fill with concern but mirth over his nickname for me. I like that he thinks I'm spunky. It makes me want to be, so I say, "I'm sorry, sir. Yes, I'm scared my punishment is going to hurt, but I'm more upset because you said I disappointed you."

Storm's head tilts, and he studies me for a moment before running a soothing hand over the top of my head. "This is going to hurt me to do as much as it's going to hurt you, but I'm afraid there is no choice. Now show me what you did that made your teacher report you."

I lift my chin and square my shoulders, but I don't move to take my coat off just yet.

"Stalling is another way to make your punishment harsher, Miss Tyler. Show me, or I'll do what Mr. Roland reported and help you along."

When I remain in place, Storm slips his large hands between my belt and coat at the dip of my back. "He said your hands started back here, then slowly traced the fabric to the knot in the front. Is this how you did it?"

I nod.

Storm growls. "Use your mouth and speak, Miss Tyler. While you still can without something in it."

My heart rate soars at the promise of his cock stretching my lips and sliding into the back of my throat until I choke.

"Yes, sir. I untied the knot and showed Mr. Roland my tits with my nipples that were so hard for him." I raise my hands and lift my breasts as I say this.

"Are they hard now? For me, Miss Tyler, are those nipples hard for me?"

"Yes, sir."

Slap.

His hand burns when it cracks on my already sore ass.

"Such a naughty girl. I didn't realize how badly you needed to be taught this lesson. Had I known, we would have done this much sooner."

"Oh," I moan, then jump at his next slap.

"Brace yourself on the desk, Miss Tyler."

He stands behind me to push my hands further away from my body so I'm more stretched than braced on my desk. Then he pushes the coat off my shoulders and down my arms before his lips find my neck for a wet, open-mouthed kiss. "I love the way you taste...everywhere. But if you take this punishment like a good girl, I'm going to taste you in my favorite spot. Do you want that, Miss Tyler, hmm? Do you want my mouth on that hot little cunt?"

"Yes, sir."

Crack.

"Hmm, wrong answer. You should be worried about what I want, not what you want. We'll have to work on that."

Storm lets his hands trail down my arms as he brings the coat with them.

I bite my lower lip between my teeth when I feel the cool air on my exposed skin.

Storm leaves me standing naked and exposed, stretched so my ass is presented for him, and he walks around the back of my desk to open a drawer. Rifling around, it takes a minute to find what he's looking for. When he does, he shows me the ruler, then slaps it against his palm, making a sharp sound that has me cringing.

Coming to stand behind me once more, he parts my legs, moving my right a few inches behind my left. "Leave them like this and hold the desk. This is going to sting, Miss Tyler, but this is what happens when girls are naughty for their teachers."

Storm covers my back with his front, grips my chin, and forces me to make eye contact. Stepping out of character, he says, "Charlie, if it's too much, use red."

"Okay."

"Good girl. Trust me?"

"Yes."

Back in the role of headmaster, his hands land on my hips, and he tilts them until I'm in the exact position he wants.

My knuckles are already turning white from the hard grip I have on the lip of my desk, and he hasn't struck me yet.

Then I hear the whoosh of the ruler a split-second before it feels like fire ants on my ass.

"Fuck!" I cry. "Shit. Sorry, but that hurt."

Storm chuckles. "That's the point. If you enjoy your punishment too much, it will only encourage the unwanted behavior."

"I know how behavior modification works."

"Your mouth shouldn't be working at all right now."

I nod, my head bobbing up and down because I know he's right. But that's something Charlie knows and would say, not Miss Tyler, the naughty little schoolgirl who is in her headmaster's office getting a spanking for being a bad girl. "Sorry."

Another crack of fire spreads across one cheek, then the other before the first is lit up again.

Storm's rough palm strokes my globes as he praises me for my bravery. "You're taking this very well, Miss Tyler. Only a few more, then we'll have a little break to check on you."

The next slaps feel like bullets ripping through my flesh, and I scream after each one, tears falling from my eyes as I sob. "I'm sorry. I'll be a good girl from now on."

I hear the clank of the ruler hit the floor. Turning a second before Storm cups my breasts in his large palms, his thumbs drawing circles around each peak, making them pull tighter, I exhale.

He lifts one breast as he lowers his head to take the nipple into his mouth.

I expect him to lave it and bring me comfort after the pain he just brought to my ass, but instead, he bites down hard, then pulls until my head falls back and his name leaves my lips.

He switches to the other and I swear I'm losing my mind.

It hurts.

Everything hurts.

My ass is on fire, my nipples feel like they've been torn off, but yet, I don't think I've ever been more wet in my life.

"That's my brave girl. Doing so well. All done for now. Let's have a look at how much you liked that."

Storm falls to his knees, bringing his face level with my ass with a male groan. His palms cup my cheeks, and he squeezes until I moan. "Fuck! This ass, Miss Tyler. I want it. Do you understand what I mean by that? I want to fuck this ass. Watch it swallow up my cock as I pound into you."

"Sir, I've never done that."

"Jesus. That makes me want it even more. But this isn't the time or place. We need to work up to that."

He spreads my ass and plunges his tongue between my globes, licking and biting as his hands pull my thighs further apart and rub my arousal over them.

"You're so fucking wet, Miss Tyler. Drenched, if I'm being honest. Were you this wet for Mr. Roland?"

"No, sir, only for you."

Another growl fills the room. Then Storm's tongue lashes at my pussy from behind.

Pulling back, he says, "Because you took that punishment so well, I'm going to give you a reward then we're going to take a picture of this red, welted ass and send it to Mr. Roland, so he knows you've been dealt with."

Storm sits on the floor, the back of his head against my desk and his mouth covering my clit. He licks and sucks until I can't take another second, and my hips grind into his face.

"That's my girl. Take what you need to make it feel good. Use my face, my scruff, my tongue. Come in my mouth, baby."

"Storm," I cry as my climax threatens to wreck me. "Sir, may I come for you? Now? I'm going to come now."

Storm growls into my pussy, then nods his head. "Go ahead. Come for me."

I break apart into a million pieces right before his eyes. My hands try their best to keep their grip on the desk, but when my knees give out, I can't hold myself upright, and I fall to the floor.

Storm brings his mouth to my temple and murmurs words of adoration and praise until I'm squirming for his belt.

Reaching for it, I unlatch the buckle and rip the zipper down.

"Something I can help you with, Miss Tyler?"

"I want your cock, sir. I want to feel it."

"Your wish is my command. Take it out, Miss Tyler, it's all yours."

My fingers wrap around his girth, and I give him a squeeze.

"Have you done this to a man before?"

"Only once, sir. Am I doing it right?"

Storm moans when I move my hand up his shaft, then back down again, twisting my wrist with each stroke. When my fingers stroke over the head of his dick, Storm sucks in a deep inhale of air. "I want to shoot my load on your tits. Spanking you...Jesus, Charlie. I almost shot all over your ass after the first slap."

"Storm," I cry. If he's calling me Charlie, I'm taking that as a sign we're out of our game. "Yes, I want to make you come."

He rests his forehead against mine and looks down to watch his cock throbbing in my hand. Resting between my breasts, he rocks his hips in time with my fist. He brings his hands to the sides of my breasts then squeezes them together, capturing his cock in between. His eyes meet mine for a brief beat, then he collects saliva in his mouth and spits on his length.

"So slick. Fucking these tits until I come. Watch." He rambles until his pace falters, his head falls back, and he roars like an animal.

His dick thickens, then pulses through his orgasm, spurting his cum on my breasts.

Storm's eyes dilate as he sees his release coating my flesh. He reaches out with one lone finger to run it through the substance, then swirls it where it's collecting in the divot of my throat.

Bringing his coated finger to my mouth, I open for him and moan when his taste hits my tongue.

He snarls. "Let me tell you what's going to happen now." He grinds his substantial length—even as he grows flaccid—against me, then rocks his hips for more friction. "I'm going to take you to bed wherever we can find one and take care of you. Hold you all night. Show you how much you allowing me to do this means to me."

Storm

With her taste still on my tongue and her scent on my fingers, Charlie is pliant in my arms as I cradle her in my lap. I did her wrong last time without giving her the aftercare I wanted to provide. I won't make that mistake again. "I need to take care of you, baby. We play hard. You need care and comfort after taking all that. Can we stay here for a bit, then we'll go to sleep? If you're tired, you can sleep here in my arms for a while."

"M-kay."

Charlie rests her head on my shoulder, and I plant a gentle kiss to her temple, then her cheek and last her nose. "Charlie, you're so beautiful, and I am so proud of you. You're already where it takes newbies months to get."

"You're an excellent teacher," she whispers with closed eyes. "I can't explain why I feel so comfortable with you already. It's like I've known you forever. Like this is what sex is supposed to be. I always wanted it to be like this, but I knew none of the other men I was with would understand, so I just accepted sex as meh, and wishfully watched porn to get off."

I smile into her neck. "You smell like me."

"Mmm. I like the way you smell."

"I'm going to put you on the sofa for a minute so I can get something to clean you up. Do you have any lotion? I'm sure your ass could use a gentle rubbing."

"Sounds nice. In the bathroom cabinet. I keep my hand cream and body lotion in there. You can use whichever."

I ease her from my lap onto the cushion, then retrieve what I need from her en suite.

Returning to her office, I ease a soapy washcloth over her skin to clean her of my orgasm, then run it between her legs.

Once clean, I dry her skin then instruct her to lie on her belly so I can treat her ass.

With lotion on my palms, I massage the thick cream into her flesh and can't help the pinging of pride in my chest when she flinches at the sting of my touch, then eases into the cushion with a satisfied sigh.

"Sore?"

"Yeah, but in a good way. I'm not sure I'll want a spanking for the next week, but once it's not so raw, I'd like to do it again."

A smile breaks out on my face from ear to ear. "Where are you planning on us sleeping tonight?" I ask because her yawns are growing closer together, and she fights to keep her eyes open.

"The dorm for the youngest kids. They don't know the difference, if we sleep in a room together or not. Plus, there are a few empty staff rooms. When we're not at full staff capacity, it's safest for the lower ratio of adults to kids to be with the youngest residents."

"Makes sense. You ready, Spunky? You're exhausted."

"Yeah."

After I dress her, Charlie and I make our way hand in hand through the snow. I keep her body tugged tightly into mine, so she doesn't get cold.

At Moose House, the dorm for the youngest girls, Charlie swipes her key card to gain us entry. She sent a text to the housemaster when we were walking over to alert her we'd be using a room while we were snowed in. At the door to the room, she does the same with her card and opens the door.

Inside is a full-size bed that I'm happy to see. It'll be a tight fit for my body, so Charlie will have no choice but to sleep curled up to me. There's a dresser with a mirror hanging on the wall behind it, a comfortable-looking chair in a corner and an en suite.

"I'm sorry the bed is so small," Charlie says. "This might not be all that comfortable for you."

"I'll be just fine with your naked body pressed against mine, don't you worry."

Charlie giggles. "We'll see if you're still saying that in the morning when you can't turn your neck."

"I'll be alright. Let's get some sleep."

I undress her carefully, then pull back the covers for her to climb in before I remove my clothes and lie behind her, pulling her back to my front.

"Jesus, you're always so hard."

I laugh from the pit of my stomach. "That's not always the case, Char. It's being near you that does this to my dick."

"Are you okay or...I mean, we haven't had sex. We could—"

I cut her offer for sex off with a kiss to her mouth. When I let her up for air, I say, "I want nothing more than to feel how good I know it's going to be inside you. But trust me, this isn't the place for our first time. I can tell you now, it's not going to be quiet."

Charlie giggles again. "You're probably right. I could do—"

"I'm okay. I just came all over your tits. Let me hold you, and we'll both get some much-needed rest. I'm guessing the kids need caring for tomorrow?"

"Yeah, but you don't have to do anything with them. Usually on snow days like this, whatever staff we have, takes them all into the huge gym and plays games and stuff with them. The older kids are actually really great with the younger ones."

"Sounds like fun. Maybe I can dust off my three-point shot."

"You played basketball?" She laughs. "I would have guessed football."

"Played both. What about you?" I ask as I run a hand over her arms, then snuggle her tight to me and cup her breast.

"Mmm. Sports weren't really for me. I was kind of a nerd in high school. I enjoyed reading and baking."

I groan.

"What?"

"The nerd scenario gives me ideas."

I grind my erection into the crack of her ass, and she gasps. "What you said before about there...getting me ready to take you. How exactly does that happen?"

"Interested in anal sex? Don't be ashamed of that. Many people enjoy it and have even stronger orgasms that way. I use a prostate stimulator most of the time when I jerk off for that reason."

"Oh, wow. Well, yeah. I mean, I never really gave it much thought. No one ever suggested it and I never asked, but since you mentioned it, I seem to think about it a lot."

"Charlie Tyler, I swear you were made for me. We'll talk about that when we get home. I don't have anything here or at the condo we need to get you ready. We'll do a little shopping though, okay?"

She yawns and barely agrees before her breathing slows and she falls asleep in my arms.

Waking up with Charlie wrapped around my body makes the creak in my neck and the ache in my spine well worth it. But my grumbling stomach needs food and after the way she made me come so hard on her tits, my body direly needs hydration, not to mention caffeine.

I nudge the back of her neck with my nose and inhale the scent of her shampoo. She doesn't budge.

I tease a nipple with my finger, and she barely squirms.

Flipping her gently to her back, I spread her legs and climb into the space between. Opening her pussy with my thumbs, I run my tongue up her slit, then flick her clit until her hands go into my hair.

I groan at her taste and the pain of her nails against my scalp, but my mouth doesn't falter. Without missing a beat, I lap at her entrance, eat her pussy, and suck at her clit until Charlie reaches for her pillow and covers her face to muffle her cries as she comes for me.

"Oh, my god!" she moans. "If I could wake up like that every morning, I probably wouldn't hate exercising at the crack of dawn so much."

"Baby, it'd be my pleasure to wake you up every day, but even though eating that pussy is my favorite meal, I'm starving and need actual food. You can have the bathroom first, but don't take long. I'm not nice when I'm hungry."

Charlie bats my arm. "Well, if that wasn't being nice, then I guess I like you mean."

I smack her ass as she climbs out of bed.

While she's in the bathroom, my erection subsides, but he throbs out a protest when she returns.

Passing her in the doorframe on my way in to take a leak, I pull her into my arms. "I checked the weather on my phone. If they can clear the roads enough, we should be good to head out by noon. I plan to be balls deep in your pussy an hour later. Gotta love the inaccuracy of the weather people."

She visibly shivers, and I close the door to deal with pissing with a raging cock.

In the cafeteria, we find the staff busy with breakfast, but they refuse help. Lots of kids' hands are on deck and the way they smile with pride over their tasks makes my chest grow warm.

We place our order with a young girl with Down's Syndrome who asks Charlie if I'm her boyfriend.

"He's a friend who is a boy," Charlie says as she looks at me over the rim of her coffee.

"He looks all man to me, Miss T. I think he likes you."

"I do. I like Miss T a lot."

"I have a boyfriend. His name is Ryan. That's him over there."

A skinny kid, also with Down's, waves in our direction with the biggest smile for our waitress I've ever seen.

Charlie tugs the girl's hand. "Jessie, the Snowball Dance is coming up. Don't forget what I told you about a dress, okay?"

"Yes, Miss T. I remember. You're going to take me to the store, but I can't tell anyone."

Charlie and I connect glances, and I smirk.

"That's right. We'll go as soon as the snow is cleared up."

"Okay, what are you going to eat? We got eggs, bacon, waffles, or cereal. We didn't make pancakes because Wendy started crying when she couldn't use the stove." Jessie rolls her eyes, then adds with pride, "I'm allowed to use it, though."

"But you didn't make Wendy feel bad, did you?"

"No! I'm not a dipper."

I furrow a brow in confusion, and Charlie gives me the Cliff Notes version of a story about filling buckets.

"Jessie, can I have an order of everything?"

"Everything? You're going to get fat!"

"Jessie!" Charlie scolds. "Is that nice to say to a customer?"

Jessie hangs her head. "No. I'm sorry."

"It's okay," I say. "I'm a big guy. But I promise it won't make me fat. I work out a lot."

"Ohhhh." Jessie blushes. "You have muscles?"

Under her breath, Charlie mumbles, "Don't encourage her." She turns back to Jessie. "Jessie, honey, I'll have eggs and bacon with toast, okay?"

"Sure, Miss T." Then the girl does a little dance that ends in a curtsy. "Coming right up."

When we're alone, I say, "She's adorable. What's up with the dress shopping?"

Charlie sighs. "Jessie's from a wealthy family who hides her here because they think it's the dark ages and a child with a developmental disability is a disgrace. Her IQ and potential make this place totally inappropriate for her. She should be here a few weeks out of the year for her school breaks and in the mainstream the rest of the time. I've begged them to let us integrate her into the high school in town, but they refuse. They also refuse to accept she's a human being with desires and really likes Ryan. We monitor their dates and constantly talk about sex and protection. All she wants to do is look like a princess in a pretty dress and go to a dance with a boy. Like. A. Normal. Girl. They have more money than god but told her to wear what they always tell her to wear. She wants a new dress like the rest of the girls are going to have."

"So, you're taking her shopping?" I ask with a huge smile.

"I'm taking her shopping."

We spend the day hanging out with the kids, who all turn out to be pretty amazing. Even Nicky Gillespie. The kid is actually quite the basketball player. Almost beat me in a game of one on one.

Almost.

After the game, I earned respect in the kid's eyes, and he promised to stop giving Charlie a hard time provided that I promise to give him a rematch and come back whenever I can to hang out. The poor kid just wants attention from an adult male he can identify with.

By mid-afternoon, we arrive back at the condo complex to find Charlie's place had been broken into while we were gone. Whoever did it was looking for something, and they weren't neat about their search.

Her stuff is all over the place. Couch flipped over in the living space, pots and pans cover the kitchen floor, and her toiletries in the bathroom lay broken everywhere we look. But it's her bedroom where she loses it when she sees her clothes and most personal items were touched.

"They touched my panties," she cries into my chest. "And my toys. Storm, they went through all my stuff."

"I know, Spunky. It's an invasion of your privacy. Everything you're feeling right now is normal and warranted."

"Do you think it was the same people who stole my identity?"

"I'm not sure, Charlie, but I promise I'm going to keep you safe while I find out. Now, let's go to my place and I'll get you settled. Then we'll call the police. I want Callan and the guys to come and have a look first, though."

"I can't wear any of those clothes again." She bends down to collect the sex toys that were in her bedside drawer. "I don't want Callan to see these."

I stop her with a hand to her forearm. "He's is a big boy. I'm sure he's seen them all before."

"Not mine!"

It makes me chuckle. "Thank fuck for that!" I exclaim.

It works and makes Charlie finally crack the slightest of smiles. "Maybe we should take that trip to the mall today. I don't want you here while they're doing the cleanup, anyway. We can take Jessie and she can get her dress while you pick up a few things to get you by."

Her eyes meet mine. "You want to come shopping with me and Jessie?"

I smile at the pitch in her voice. She's tearing up, her emotions raw. "Yeah. I do. Now, let's get you over to my place so I can call Black."

Reaching Callan on the first ring, I look at the clock and know he must be at Spill the Tea having his afternoon treat of sugar. "Hey, we've got a problem."

"Where are you?"

"My condo, but I've got female company. Don't want to say anymore over the phone."

Black emits a deep laugh. "You think anyone is smarter than me and can get past all the security I have on our lines?"

"Still," I say. "Better safe than sorry."

"Okay, okay, okay. Let me finish my snack—"

I interrupt to keep him honest. "You mean dessert."

"I know what I mean. I'll grab the others and we'll see you in thirty. I'll text you when we're in the lot. Come out."

With that, he's gone, and I turn my attention to the girl wrapped in a throw blanket on my sofa with a warm mug of tea in her hands.

Charlie

My nerves are shot to shit when I call Rourke and fill him in on what's transpired.

I call because I need him to know what's going on, but also because I'm scared to be alone.

I lied to Storm. I told him I was fine, and he should go outside alone to talk to his friends.

I know Callan, Ace, and Elliot work with him. We've all known the three Falls Village residents did something other than eat sweets at Colleen's place and run a bed-and-breakfast and restaurant. This confirms my suspicions that they work undercover in some capacity and therefore, so must Storm.

"Are you alone?"

"No. Well, yes, at the moment, but I'm fine. I'm at Storm's. He had to go outside for a minute."

I don't tell him Storm is outside with Callan Black, Ace Lyons, and Elliot Montgomery filling them in on the whole story of my identity theft that I finally finished sharing with him when we first arrived at his place after finding my condo ransacked.

"Okay," Rourke says with a deep exhale. "Why didn't you tell any of us this was to this level and dangerous? We figured it was a silly little stolen credit card thing."

I sigh. I didn't want to worry anyone. I'm the one in charge. I'm supposed to be strong and handle everything on my own, not need to go crying to my friends, or now the big, powerful man in my life to save me and make everything better. But hell, does it feel good to relinquish some of that control to Storm and know I'm safe with him.

The need to sink into his safe arms and bury my face in the scent at his neck is overwhelming. How this man became my comfort, my oxygen this fast is unexplainable, but here we are.

"I didn't want to worry you guys," I admit. "Plus, honestly, I sort of thought the same thing. Dan Buzzle did, too."

"He's not the sharpest knife in the drawer, Char."

"Yeah, I know. Anyway, when Storm is done with what he's doing, we're going to call him. We need to let the police know. I don't want to be here when they're going through everything. Knowing strangers looked through my belongings is enough. I don't need to be present when the police see it all, too."

"Come here," he offers.

"Thanks, but Storm and I are actually going to take Jessie to the mall for her dress and so I can get new clothes. I'm not wearing the ones they touched."

I shiver at the thought of them touching my panties, or maybe doing more. No way are those ever going on my body again.

Rourke sighs. "Her parents still refusing to send her a new dress?"

"Yup."

"Have you spoken to Montana? I saw her contract, so I know she's coming next week."

"Exactly why I didn't call her. She'd only get upset and say something to her parents, who will then slap my hands over confidentiality. Once Montana is here, she'll see for herself. She warned her parents last time, if this continued, she was going to file for custody. I hope she does. I have enough documentation to help her win the case."

Rourke and I finish up with a quick rundown of the events of the snowstorm and how the kids were during mine and Storm's stay. Just as we're saying goodbye, Storm walks through his door and comes straight to where I'm sitting.

"Hey."

"Hi. Everything okay?"

Storm's hand finds the back of his neck. "You know I can only say so much. You're a smart cookie, so I know you've figured a bit out. Callan, Ace, and Elliot are going to sweep and process your apartment for me. Once they've done that, Ace and Elliot will leave, and Black and I will call the police. When they get here, Black will deal with them, and I'll take you and Jessie to the mall. By the time we're back, your condo will be like new."

"I don't want to stay there."

A smile breaks out on his face, half happy, the rest sad. "I wouldn't think of it. You're staying here with me. Make me a list later and I'll go over there to get whatever you want after the mall, okay?"

I nod. "Thanks."

I cuddle into his chest, burying my face with a sigh as his scent fills my lungs.

Storm brushes a hand over my head, smoothing my hair. "Go take a hot shower. You'll smell like me, but I like that. Tonight, you can take a bath with your own things. We'll go get Jessie when you're ready."

I nod and stretch up on my tiptoes to plant a soft swipe of my lips over his. "Thank you."

It doesn't take Jessie over five seconds to get ready when Storm and I show up and surprise her with a trip to the mall. She climbs in the car and warns Storm to buckle up and stay within the speed limit, and I already feel the smile split my face and the tension of the day's earlier events seep away.

At the mall, Jessie finds the perfect bubblegum pink gown and Storm brings tears to my eyes when he sneaks off and buys a matching tie and vest for Ryan, so he'll match his date. But then he insists on buying my new panties and bras, knowing I can't make too much of a fuss with Jessie here. He also adds in a few pieces of his choosing, which makes it hard to be mad at him, knowing he's got plans for us later.

When we get back to the camp, Jessie nearly catapults herself out of the moving vehicle. She's so excited to bring Ryan his surprises. "Can I go to Ryan's dorm now, please?" she begs with wide eyes as she bounces on her toes.

I glance at the time on my phone and know before I see it that allowing this is breaking another rule. But being the rules are technically mine, I smile and nod. "Sure."

Jessie tugs Storm along and reaching the boys' dorm, she yells Ryan's name at the top of her ample lungs, nearly shattering my eardrum.

"Jessie, hush. When sneaking around and breaking the rules, a girl needs to be quiet about it."

"Oh, okay, Miss T. I've never broken the rules before. I'll try to remember that rule."

Storm wraps an arm around her shoulder and cuddles her into his side. "Now, don't you go getting any ideas about breaking rules. Ask Miss T over there what happens to naughty girls."

"Storm!" I scold, but can't help the smile when he wiggles his eyebrows over Jessie's head.

I swipe my card and let us into the building. Thankfully, that's excitement enough for Jessie to forget Storm's comment.

But I don't. Leaning in, I say, "Headmaster, I'm sorry for breaking into the boys' dorm after dark. Don't punish me too harshly."

Storm growls and shifts himself in his pants. "Damn, woman. You know how to make a guy rise for the occasion."

I giggle and bump him with my hip. "Thank you for distracting me."

"You doing okay, Spunky?" he asks.

I nod. "Yeah, I am. I still need that bath you promised, though."

"As soon as we get home. Callan texted me earlier. The guys grabbed your toiletries and put them in my condo."

"Oh. That was nice of them, I guess. What's a few more guys touching my stuff, right?"

"Hey," he scolds. "I'm the only guy touching anything of importance that belongs to you."

That brings the smile back to my face as I cup his in my palm. "I like that."

"Me, too, Charlie. Me, too."

Ryan's excited laughter fills the hallway over his three rule-breaking guests. "What you all doing here? Miss T, Jessie is not allowed here after dark."

"I know, but we have a surprise for you, and it's okay because Mr. Roland and I are with her."

"He bought you these," Jessie says and shoves the bag into Ryan's hands. "They match me, so we'll be the same."

Not understanding what she's talking about, Ryan rips open the bag and his face falls. "What are these? I'm a boy. I don't like pink."

Jessie looks about ready to cry when Storm swoops in and yet again saves the day. "Ryan, my man. Listen up, dude. These are things you'll wear to the dance, so you and Jessie will match. It's one of those guy things we have to accept. The ladies pick the color of their dresses, and we just have to match them. But I saw your girl in her gown, and she looked beautiful. Why don't you tell her you can't wait to see her in it."

"I can't wait to see you in it," Ryan says, then adds, "But I wish it was red. Red is my favorite color."

Storm chuckles. "Jessie mentioned that, so here." Storm hands him a small bag he was hiding in his coat. "See if this is cool."

Ryan opens the bag and pulls out a pocket square. It's pink, but the roses are red. The best of both worlds for these two and it nearly causes my heart to explode in my chest. My ovaries had no chance. They were goners hours ago when he showed us the vest and tie.

Ryan is much happier now that he has something red to wear, and Jessie makes me proud when she uses her negotiating skills we're always working on and says, "I'll wear red to the prom at the end of the school year, Ryan." But then her eyes turn sad and meet mine. "If my mom and dad will send me a red one."

"Hey," I say, pulling her into my arms. "Don't worry. Montana will be here for that dance, and you know how much she likes to shop."

Jessie fist bumps the air and says, "Oh yeah! Girl's day at the mall. You'll come, too, Miss T."

"Of course."

After getting a very overtired and overly excited Jessie back to her dorm and situated for her nightly routine, Storm and I head to his truck.

We don't make it three streets when the snow starts up again.

"Man, you get a lot of snow up here, huh?"

I laugh. "It's winter in Maine."

Storm slams on the brakes and braces my body with his muscular forearm. "Fuck! And right on cue is a motherfucking big-ass moose."

The moose stands about seven feet tall, sporting dark brown fur and a shoulder hump. He must weigh over a thousand pounds. Living here all these years, they're still a sight to see. "Oh, my!" I exclaim as Storm puts the truck in park and we watch in collective awe as the majestic beast crosses in front of us.

"An icon of the Maine woods, they're name means bark stripper," I state. Storm is still silent. "Say something."

"I'm just happy right now that they're herbivores."

That elicits a deep chuckle from me. "But I'm not."

Storm's huge palm squeezes my knees. "Is that so?"

"That's so. I like meat. Know where I can find any?"

"I got your meat right here, baby," Storm says with a youthful smile while grabbing his hardening bulge.

Setting the truck back into drive, we watch as the moose disappears into the forest, and we make our way back to human society and our condo complex where the story of my apartment's break-in has reached my friends and co-workers.

Huddled in parkas on my stoop with mugs of steaming beverages—I'm sure at least some of them include alcohol—are Rourke and his husband, Emily and her boyfriend, Ian and Sally, Shana, and Kayley.

"Is that a firepit on your porch?"

I shrug. "It's Kayley's. She brings it with her for warmth. She grew up in North Carolina, followed a guy here. When they ended, she stayed because she loves her job. The climate, not so much."

Storm nods and puts the truck in park. "Rourke told them about the break-in."

"Yeah. That's what I'm guessing, too."

He climbs out of the cab after shooting me a warning glance not to move until he's come around to my side. Opening my door, Storm takes my hand and leads me to my crew of supportive, if not nosey, friends.

"Hey everyone," I say. "Having a fire?"

Kayley wraps her arms around me and checks me over for injuries I couldn't have sustained from a break-in that occurred while I wasn't there, but I appreciate the gesture all the same.

Before I have the strength—her concern feels too good to push away—to move out of her grip, Sally is in my ear, promising she'll color with me when we get inside. Sally is convinced if adults would just color, they wouldn't need medication to survive adulting. It doesn't sound all that awful now.

Feeling left out, Shana drags my body to hers for a hug as she hums a soothing tune into my free ear.

"Hey!" Emily scolds. "I'm the trained psych around here and her closest and dearest friend."

The rest roll their eyes at her dramatics but allow her into the fold as I hear the men asking Storm for details.

With one ear on the male conversation happening about me, I melt when I hear Storm declare me as his and promise the other men I'm safe in his care.

"I'm staying at Storm's," I say. "So can we move this over there? I kind of don't want to be here right now."

Ushering everyone a few feet to Storm's we abandon the outside festivities for his warm living room fire. Food is ordered and delivered before I have the chance to play hostess. I only realize it's happened when Storm places the plate on my lap with pizza and salad. "Oh. Thanks. You ordered food?"

Storm brushes it off with a shrug. "Figured you were hungry. We never ate dinner. Shopping can wipe a girl out. Or so my sister-in-law and niece are always saying."

I smile and tug him down to my lips. "You're really amazing, you know that?"

"I try." His smile beams through the room brighter than the embers from the crackling fire.

Rourke plops down next to me on the sofa and places his warm palm on my knee with a gentle pat. "Hey," he says with a smile for Storm. "You holding up okay? No bullshit, just between us."

I shrug. "I don't know. It helped to go shopping and see how excited Jessie was about her new dress, and Storm bought Ryan a matching vest and tie."

Rourke's face fills with adoration for the newcomer to our group. "Did you?" he asks.

Storm shrugs it off like it was nothing when it was so much.

"You don't have to pretend to not be scared, Char," Rourke says. "Fuck, I'm scared for you. Don't get mad at me, but I think we should add security on campus until this blows over."

"I agree. I'll call Black."

"Black?" Rourke asks Storm. "You mean Callan Black?"

Storm clears his throat. "Yeah."

The meaning of their connection isn't lost on Rourke or the others listening to our exchange.

"Friend of yours?" Ian asks.

"Yeah."

"Callan is a huge supporter of the camp," Rourke helpfully supplies to take away the suspicion emanating from the others. "He was close with Charlie's dad. Attended the camp years ago as a troubled teen and never forgot about the place. When he had the means to do so, he started sending checks. Once he moved up here, we asked him to sit on the board." Rourke chuckles. "It makes for much more interesting meetings."

Storm bellows. "I bet. Love the guy, but he can be...a lot."

"When my dad passed, he told me he was more of a father figure to him than his own dad ever was."

The people in the room who knew my dad take a private minute to remember the man whose dream it was to provide what we do for our students and their families.

"Speaking of...a lot." Emily clears her throat. "Charlie, you've been through a traumatic experience. Being robbed, having someone go through your things, is an invasion of privacy. I think you need to talk about it. Process your feelings."

We collectively roll our eyes.

"I did Sally's coloring sheets."

"You're not letting go of the feelings though. You're trying to control them like you do everything else. You're not experiencing them."

"She lets go when it counts," Storm says, and all eyes widen.

I cover my face with my hands, then peep out through a slit in my fingers.

"Well." Ian chuckles. "Maybe she just needed the right man."

"I agree," Storm states.

"Wait, did I miss something?" Shana asks. "We're talking about sex, right? And Charlie letting go of control?"

"Um...no, I don't want to talk about sex and my holding or letting go of anything."

Storm laughs. "She holds on to it as well as she lets go."

The men fist bump like children, and the women smirk at their immature nature.

Our resident psychologist pipes up again. "It's nothing to be embarrassed about. We all have and enjoy sex. Some of us like to be dominant during it, others like to be dominated. Take Ian and Sally for example—"

"Hey!" Ian scolds. "No, don't take Ian and Sally into consideration as anything." He turns toward Sally. "Why does she know anything about our sex life?"

Sally lifts a shoulder. "I don't know. She's a shrink—"

"School psychologist," we all quickly clarify, only to have Emily roll her eyes our way.

"Same thing," Emily demands.

"Not really," Brad, Rourke's husband adds. He's a quiet man, so when anything comes from his mouth, people tend to listen. "What? It's technically not exactly the same."

Shana lowers her voice to a whisper to ask, "Are we talking about like chains and whips exciting us?"

I laugh, and my eyes go to Storm because where I'm not sure I'd be into getting whipped, his spankings are amazing and if those chains are fur lined handcuffs making me immobile to his evil advances, count me in.

"Ohh." Rourke rubs his palms on his thighs. "I saw that look."

I blush feverishly red. "What look? Stop making this into something."

"I'm not making this into anything. Like Emily said, we're all having sex and—"

Kayley groans. "Speak for yourself. My vibrator died at the worst possible time last night."

"Maybe you need a guy like Storm. I bet Charlie's toys are at their fullest charge."

"Nah," Storm says, then winks my way. "Even guys like me use them. They're the best for orgasm denial."

"Why does that sound amazing and like torture at the same time?" Shana asks.

"Because it is," Brad supplies and all eyes shift to him and Rourke.

Rourke clears his throat, pats his thighs, and declares the night over. "We should all head out and leave Charlie and Storm. She needs her rest."

"I don't think that's what she's about to get."

I yawn, and my friends get the clue that it's time for them to head to their units and leave Storm and me to get to more intimate activities.

Storm ushers the crew to the door as I clean up the few items left behind before we meet up in the kitchen. As I'm loading the dishwasher, his breath on my neck is warm and full of promises I'm planning on holding him to. "You mentioned something about a bath. How about I start, and you join me in a few minutes?"

"Anything you want. The guys said your stuff is in the bathroom. Make yourself at home."

I brush a hand over his strong biceps, then stretch on my toes for a gentle kiss. "Give me like ten minutes."

Storm wraps a hand around my waist and tugs me to his side. "Char, I'm not sure tonight is the right time for what I want to do to you." His hand moves to surround my throat, and he squeezes, his eyes locked to mine to gauge when his hold hits the sweet spot, not too tight, but tight enough it gives me the mindfuck of him choking me. "I'm not sure how easy I'll be able to go our first time."

He releases my throat, then licks up the side of my neck.

I giggle as I lift my shirt over my head and drop it at his feet. "Good. I'm not in the mood for gentle tonight either."

I feel his eyes on me as I walk to his bedroom, stepping out of my pants and leaving them on the floor. Shaking my ass as I lower my panties, I hear Storm's growl before I reach the hallway. "Take care of what you need fast, little girl. Daddy isn't feeling very patient tonight."

Storm

I'm convinced I'm insane as I give Charlie her few minutes of privacy in the tub before I march in there. Then again, maybe because, like a nutcracker on Christmas Eve, this woman was breaking the shell that's hardened around my heart.

I wasn't always the guy who slept around, not wanting anything serious. Nope. That all started right before I left for bootcamp, and Lynn crushed me.

Lynn was the girl I thought of as the love of my life until very recently.

I met Lynn senior year of college, and we had a whirlwind romance. Met at a party on Thursday, were living together by Sunday. That was the official move our stuff together day, but in all honesty, we went home together on Thursday night and never parted ways.

And that's how we stayed for eight months.

Then, as graduation loomed nearer and Lynn received the job offer of her dreams in California, things changed.

She grew distant and cold. Started shutting me out of her life, no longer spoke to me about her hopes and dreams. It was as if all of hers were falling into place and they no longer included me.

Then one night, ironically, at the same frat house party where we first met, I walked in and instantly knew something was wrong. Even before my training in the military, my senses were heightened for trouble, and I found it that night.

Lynn and one of the hockey players walked out of a bedroom right in front of my face. There was no denying what they'd been doing in there. Not that either of them tried.

In the dude's defense, he at least had the decency to act clueless about her relationship status and tried to offer me an apologetic shrug. Lynn, on the other hand, wiped the corner of her mouth with her finger, then knowingly smirked at me.

Of course, a fight ensued, and I found myself sleeping in my car. I enlisted the following morning.

After packing my shit, I went back to the house we shared. I spent the better part of the night drunk leaving her nasty messages on our answering machine. The joint outgoing message made me sick each time I heard our mingled sing-song voices.

The next day was graduation, but the school was so huge, I didn't see Lynn. I sent her one last fuck you send off message, then left and never looked back.

But I'm not that stupid twenty-two-year-old douche bag who lashed out when his ego was bruised instead of asking what went wrong. I'm a grown ass man who thought he was set enough in his ways that his heart was safe from women.

I was wrong because Charlene Tyler found a way past the layers that have been in place for half my life.

In only a few days, Charlie made each of mine brighter. She's changed me from a lonely man pretending the girls in his bed—who were too young for him—were enough into a man who wants nothing more but to take care of the woman soaking in a tub in the next room.

I enter the bathroom, and my breathing falters at the sight of the woman in front of me.

Charlie's eyes are covered by the relaxing mask Elliot's wife sent for her after hearing about the break-in. With ear buds in place, she doesn't hear me enter.

I stand immobile and watch this amazing woman who is becoming my everything faster than is sensible for a man with my experience. She makes me feel things I wasn't sure I'd ever be able to again. But here I am with a smile on my face as she shifts in the bubbles, and it's not only because her movements expose a peaked nipple.

Sure, the beauty of her face and body mesmerizes me into a state I can only describe as dazed and confused, but it's so much more with this woman who I was sent to investigate.

How things can shift in the blink of an eye.

Charlie stretches and the column of her elegant neck makes my mouth water as a craving to collar her hits me.

I've never understood the Doms at the clubs I've been to who prance around with their subs adorned in collars. I always saw it as more of a pissing contest, a conquest won over the others. Now, I understand their need to claim their woman so no other man would dare to look their way.

My heart swells in my chest when I think of her as mine, wearing a chocker around her throat to symbolize our bond. The image of a ring on her finger isn't far behind. When the idea of her belly expanding with my child fills my thoughts, I know I'm fucked.

Surprising her with a sweep of my lips over hers, she whimpers into my mouth and my need for her grows in my heart as much as my aching cock.

"Storm," she purrs, and it sounds like a prayer on her lips even to this non-religious man. But if anyone can make me be a believer, it's this woman. I'd worship at the temple of Charlie Tyler every day of my life.

The water sloshes over the edge of the tub when she shifts to reach for me.

Pulling me to her wetness, I groan when she soaks my shirt.

Reaching behind my body, I fist my collar and yank the garment off in one motion, then lift her into my arms.

Grabbing a fluffy towel from the hanger on the back of the door, I lay it over her body then march toward my bed, where I place her on the sheets. They'll need to be changed after what I have planned for us anyway, what's a little water?

I dry her as best as my patience will allow, then dip to taste her in that spot where her neck meets her shoulder and the sound Charlie makes has my cock bouncing in my pants, pleading with me to let him out.

My tongue finds her weak spot behind her ear as my fingers weave through her hair. "Charlie," I whisper. "Are you going to be Daddy's good girl, or should I prepare myself for a punishment before I fuck you?"

She sucks in a gulp of air as I kiss along her jaw, then sink inside her mouth for a long kiss.

When need takes over, I let us come up for air then state, "Baby, you're so fucking amazing. Tell me your pussy is wet for me."

"Yes."

"Yes?" I prompt.

"Yes, Daddy. My pussy is wet for only you."

"Good girl," I praise, then lower my mouth to capture the rose bud nipple that tastes like sugar on my tongue.

Pulling it in between my teeth, she arches her back. "Storm," she cries. "I want you so much. Please."

My heart bursts in my chest when her eyes set on mine and hold my stare. Then she asks, "What is this? For you, I mean. What is this for you?"

"Everything, Charlie. Everything and then more."

I slide my tongue along the seam of her lips, and she parts them for me.

"I want you to make love to me. Please, make love to me first, before you fuck me like a naughty girl."

"Yeah." I sigh. "Yeah, I want that, too. Jesus, I don't know what you've done to me, but I so fucking want that."

I kiss her long and hard and savor every second of her naked under me, her hips pushing up into my erection as she seeks relief at my hands.

I sit up on my knees and yank down my jeans and boxers. As she watches my cock spring, she licks her lips. "Behave," I admonish. "or I'm going to have no choice but to fuck you good and hard first, then make love to you and that's not what either of us wants, is it?"

"No, Daddy," she sasses.

I moan because of her attitude, but more because she wraps her soft hand around the base of my shaft and squeezes me in her grip.

All restraint has vacated the premises.

I place myself atop her and bracket her body with each hand.

Charlie turns her head and licks my bicep. The wetness from her mouth should cool my skin, but instead it's like a flame.

With eyes overflowing with so many emotions I can't identify, I say her name. "Charlene."

"You've never called me that before."

I smile. "First time for a few things. I've also never felt like this for a woman before or wanted to bring emotions into the act of fucking. And yes, that's all I'm usually into. Fucking. Maybe just some plain old sex now and then, but wanting to mix up feelings in the bed and make love to a woman? Nah. This is a first for me, baby."

She nods in what I think is understanding, then asks, "Protection?"

"Shit. Let me get—"

"I'm on the pill and clean. I swear. I haven't been with a man in a really long time."

While she strokes my dick, I groan. "I'm clean, and I trust you."

"Okay, good."

"Yeah."

I let my head slip back and gnash my teeth together to stave off my need to come from the ministrations of her hand alone. "Open your legs for me. I need to be inside you, feel you."

"Yes."

Charlie spreads for me. She's wet and swollen, ready to be taken gently or hard, and if I have my way, she'll allow me both before this night is over.

"You're nice and ready for me, aren't you?"

"Yes. I need you. Want you inside me. Now. Please."

I let my hand wander down her smooth skin where I find her pussy soaking wet and ready for me to take. "Jesus! Fuck, you're so wet."

"Yes. Please."

I slide two thick fingers inside her, spread them, and shift my throbbing erection on her thigh.

Charlie arches. "Ah," she moans. "Inside me, Storm. I need you."

Hearing those words finally breaks me and I thread my fingers into her hair and bring her lips to mine. Spreading them with my tongue, she lets me in and I sweep through her, our tongues entwining.

Using the top of her head for leverage, I cup her there, then allow my cock to independently find the warm heat of her wet pussy before I nuzzle inside her one inch at a time.

Letting out my pent-up breaths, I sigh when I feel her resistance. Her body needs to relax to accommodate my girth, so I lean down and take her lips again. Whispering into her mouth, I say, "God damn, you feel so fucking good. Soft and wet, so fucking tight, Charlie. So fucking wet."

My spine lights with sparks instantly, and I'll need to check myself before I come like a virgin on his first time.

Deep breaths don't save me from losing my mind, but at least they save me from embarrassing myself.

Charlie squirms.

"You okay, baby? You feel so good around me. You can take more. Here."

I push again and gain entry for another inch of my cock.

As her heat sheaths me, I groan, and my eyes force themselves shut. Opening them, I stare down at her.

Charlie parts her lips and lets out the best sound I've ever heard. It's part moan, part mewl. It's all for me. This girl is all mine.

"Mine," I growl and rear back. Pulling out to my tip, I thrust hard and bottom out.

Charlie groans as her body tightens around me and little explosions take over my body, from my brain to my heart, my dick to my soul.

"I love your dick, Storm. You're so thick and long. No one has ever reached...oh my god! Yes! Right there."

My last resolve leaves and everything around me, everything inside me, changes in this moment like an awakening, an epiphany, the motherfucking holy grail.

"You're perfect, Charlie. So perfect for me. This pussy was made to be mine and mine alone."

I roll my hips to rock against the spot only I have ever reached deep inside her as my heart swells with love and lust. My balls throb and I know my orgasm is about to rip through me and there will be no holding back.

Reaching between us, I stroke my thumb over her clit and demand, "Come for me, Charlie. Come with me. Eyes on me and watch me come. Watch me come inside you."

She lifts off the bed again and I fight for control as I keep my steady pace, grinding into her as my cock strums her to climax.

"I'm going to come. Storm, you're making me...may I, Daddy?"

"Oh, fuck! Go! I'm fucking coming."

I roar, groan, and rut into her like an uncouth caveman. I sound like an animal as she tightens around me and cries my name.

Charlie always comes in the most amazing way, but when I'm buried inside her like this, it's like nothing I've experienced in my life.

She shudders through her climax, her hips lifting to meet my pace as I savor every last second of mine.

When her pussy clamps down on me and her wetness seeps over my balls, I shiver and lose another part of myself to her. "Baby," I say as I push the damp, sweat soaked hair from her face. "I'm going to say something, and you don't need to respond. Just think, okay?"

She nods and I lower my weight to her body, collapsing on her as I say the next words. "I'm very quickly falling in love with you."

She tries to speak, but I silence her with a finger on her lips. "Shh, no. Just think about those words for now. I'm going to pull out, then I'm going to fuck you into this mattress like the naughty little girl you are. Get on your knees for Daddy and lift that ass into the air."

She does as I demand, and I'm hard at the sight of her before I go flaccid.

Reaching into the bedside table, I grab the tube of lube and pop the cap. The sound has Charlie turning to me with wide, concerned eyes.

I smile. "You're not ready to take me here just yet, Spunky. But we're going to work on remedying that. Nice and slow, okay? Trust me?"

She nods.

That wordless response earns her a good crack on the meaty part of her ass.

"Excuse me?" I ask.

"Yes."

Crack.

"Yes what?"

"Yes, Daddy. I trust you."

Rubbing the sting away, I lean down, covering her back, and growl in her ear. "So perfect."

As I nibble on her lobe, I coat my fingers in lube, then run them through her pussy to further coat them in our combined releases.

"I'm going to fuck you hard. Like this," I state. "From behind, with you on your knees. I'm not going to stop until I've come so deep inside you, you taste my cum. And while I'm doing that, I'm going to finger your ass. In and out. With two, maybe three fingers. Spreading them until this tight asshole is ready to take my cock. Tell me you want that."

"I want that. I want you in my ass, Daddy. Please. Do it. Do it now."

"Who makes the orders?"

"I'm...I'm sorry. You. I'm just excited. I can't help it."

"Just excited?" I ask as I drizzle lube down the crack of her ass.

She moans. "Maybe a little scared, too."

I chuckle. "Can't say I blame you, but I'd never do something to you I haven't experienced. Trust me, anal sex will feel so fucking good. You'll crave my cock there all the time."

She looks over her shoulder at me and I see the question on her face, and it makes me laugh again. "I'm straight. Never been with a man. During my time at a club, I was introduced to a woman who fucked my ass with a dildo so I could experience it. She taught me the right way to go about the process, so it would be pleasurable not only to me, but to my partners as well. True Doms, the good ones, all believe they shouldn't expect something from their sub they don't understand. How else do we understand what things are like if we don't experience them?"

"So you're a Dom?" she asks. "Like in the romance books I read? I mean, I see it. It makes sense. The need for control, the Daddy kink, wanting to open my car door, and take everything on so I can relax."

"Yes, I'm a Dom by training. I'm not sure what goes on in your books, but I've done the work to be safe with others in the lifestyle. I've played in a club in New York City, but I haven't had a woman I've called my sub."

"Do you think of me like that?"

I run a hand down her back to her ass. "Yes. Are you good with that?"

Charlie hums.

"Words," I demand. "Words, open and honest communication is a must. I can't assume or make guesses about how you're feeling."

"Yes. Yes, I want you to think of me like that."

"And when we're playing, I'm your Dom?" I ask. "But only then?"

Charlie groans this time. "No, not only then. I like the way you take care of me."

"I'm good with that."

She offers me a nod. She's sinking into a sub state where my voice alone can lull her to euphoria.

I continue to talk about Dom life as I rim her tight entrance with the first finger. "Take a deep breath in," I order, and she obeys. "Let it out." As she does, I sink my finger inside her to the knuckle.

"Madam Stephanie taught me the pleasures of a prostate orgasm. I still use the vibe when I jack off to get the strongest orgasms. If you're a good girl, maybe I'll let you watch me next time."

Her ass puckers, and her body trembles at the thought of watching me masturbate with a dildo up my ass. "You like that idea, don't you?"

Before she can answer, I sink a second finger in and circle them.

"Storm..."

"Green? Good and just scared, or yellow and you need me to slow down?"

"I'm good. I'm...Oh! I think I can come like this. Jesus. Fuck, I'm going to come if you don't stop."

The smile splits my face, and I find a rhythm in her tightness.

Circle, thrust, thrust, circle, circle, spread.

Again and again until she's sweat soaked and writhing on the bed.

Then I lift my left hand and bring it down on her ass.

"Who's Daddy's bad girl?"

"Me, Daddy. I am. Please. Oh my god."

"Such a naughty girl with my fingers up your ass. Hold that orgasm. You'll come when told and not a second before. I want to be in my girl's tight cunt when I make her come."

I slam my cock inside her, and Charlie reaches for the headboard for purchase.

"That's right. Hold on tight, baby. This is going to be fast and..." I slam into her again. "Hard."

I pound into her, shifting the bed with my force.

Her pussy flutters around me as she tries her best to keep her climax at bay.

My fingers, three of them now, pump through her tightest spot as my cock fills her pussy.

Charlie cries out. "So full and tight. Please, Daddy, I need to come. So close."

"Almost, sweet girl. I'm right there, too. Let me enjoy watching my fingers spread this ass." I growl and slap her cheek hard.

It reddens instantly and a gush of wetness coats my cock.

"Going to fuck you there so soon. Can't wait. Mmm."

I lose my mind as my orgasm climbs up my spine, and my balls pull up tight.

"Daddy's going to pull out and come all over this tight hole. I want to feel it inside you when I fuck you there later. Come for me."

Charlie shatters around my cock, squeezing me so tight, I see stars as my climax threatens to ruin me.

Pulling out, I fist my cock and line the head up to her tight ass and come. Spurt after spurt fills her crease, drips down her cheek, and covers her back.

Collapsing onto my back, I tug Charlie into my arms and kiss her temple. "Fuck, that was so good. You're a dream come true in bed, and I care about you, Charlie. A lot."

"Me, too. But—"

"I'm not exactly sure what it means, if that's what you're about to ask. I know it means there's a lot we need to figure out, but right now, I think we both need to just stay right like this."

Charlie purrs and cuddles up to me.

Once comfortable in the spot on my chest that feels like it was made for her, Charlie's breathing evens out and mine matches hers as my eyes slide shut and I find the most restful sleep of my life.

Charlie

By the weekend of the Winter Festival, I've made myself right at home in Storm's apartment, his bed, and his life. There's still a lot we need to talk about. I continue to get the feeling there's something he's not telling me, but we've grown just as close as roommates as we have as lovers.

My apartment looks like new, and other than my issues with being there, there's no reason for me not to move back in.

But I'm not.

I'm staying with Storm.

Because I'm scared, because I don't want to be alone, and because I think I'm falling in love with him, and I don't know how long he'll be here. I want every second with him I can have.

He assures me Callan and the guys are on high alert, and Storm has yet to let me out of his sight. He's spent the week in my office at the camp, driving me there and back. The kids love him and knowing he's there, I've never had more of them popping in to just say hello. It's much better seeing them for visits than to be seeing them for scolding. It's renewed my love for my job.

And tonight, watching each of the students walk into the gym looking their best brings an ache to my heart. So many of them have such potential, if only their families had the skills to manage them correctly.

Entering the dance, I smile up at Storm. I have the most handsome date this year. Instead of going alone and getting stuck being chatted up by the sad, single fathers, Storm has my hand carefully in his as we walk around the gym to greet everyone.

I gasp when I see the beauty of the decorations that Sally tirelessly spearheaded. She went with a frozen tropics theme, and it's stunning. There are flowers covered in icicles, a frozen waterfall, lawn chairs wrapped in warm, fluffy fleece. It's amazing.

I pull her into my arms and tell her she outdid herself as Ian beams with pride over his girlfriend's artistic talents. "Sally misses New York," he supplies, and all heads turn.

"What?" I ask. "When did you live in New York?"

Sally shrugs at me but sends a glare Ian's way. "Ian!" she scolds, then turns in my direction. "I lived there after college when I worked in set design on Broadway. I left after...something happened, and I applied to art therapy programs."

With all eyes on Sally, we wait for her to elaborate. When she doesn't, Ian grabs for her hand and explains. "Sally was working late one night at the theater. She knew better than to walk out the back exit on her own, but it didn't stop her from doing it. A guy grabbed her, but luckily, one of her co-workers came out before it was too late and chased the guy off."

She is instantly in my arms. "I'm sorry. I didn't know any of this."

Sally sniffles into my shoulder. "How would you? No one here knows. I've only told Ian, but I'm glad you know now. It was time."

Releasing my hold, I stretch her out far enough to see her face, but I keep her hands in mine.

"It was pretty bad for a while. I couldn't work, wouldn't leave my apartment. I moved back home with my parents and went into therapy. From there, once I was better, I went to school for art therapy so I could help others. I always thought I'd do trauma patients similar to me, but one internship with kids with special needs and I was sold. Now, here I am."

A huge smile splits my face. "And I couldn't be happier to have you."

"Thanks," Sally says as she wipes under her eyes. Then she gasps and we all turn to see what's making her beam with excitement.

Jessie and Ryan walk hand in hand in their coordinating outfits through the room with confidence my staff works tirelessly for. They don't stop strutting until they're standing in front of Storm and me, Sally, and Ian.

"Hi. Don't we look great?" Jessie asks.

"You look better than great," Storm says. "You're the most beautiful girl in here with that smile on your face."

Jessie glows at the compliment, then giggles. "Mr. Roland. You're going to make Miss T mad. You're her boyfriend. You need to tell her you're sorry for saying that to me."

"No he don't, Jessie. That's giving a compiement. That's 'llowed ."

"Oh, yeah," Jessie giggles again. "I forgot."

I smirk at the lessons they're putting to good use. "But, Jessie, what should you say to Mr. Roland?"

She taps her forehead with her palm. "I forgot. Thanks, Mr. Roland."

Storm tugs her to his side for a hug. "You're welcome." Then he high fives Ryan and says, "Your date is going to be the queen of the dance, isn't she?"

Ryan nods. "And I'm the king of the world." He makes muscles with his thin arms.

Emily and Luke join our circle just as Rourke steps up onto the stage with Brad at his side to take the microphone. "Food is ready, everyone. Take your seats and let's clap for the kitchen staff that made all this yummy food tonight."

The room erupts in applause as everyone scurries for their seats.

"Gotta go," Ryan states. "Time to chow down, man!"

He tugs Jessie's hand and they run off to find their spots for dinner.

I snuggle into Storm's side. "I think you missed your calling. You're so great with them."

He kisses my temple. "I think they're pretty cool, but I couldn't do what you and the staff here do every day."

"Speaking of staff," Anita says as Storm pulls out my chair at the faculty table we've made our way to. "The rest of the extras arrive the day after tomorrow. Believe it or not, I have signed contracts from every single one of them. First time in the history of my time here."

"Which is the history of the camp," Harold needlessly adds with a kiss to his wife's cheek.

Dinner is delicious and the kids who helped create it get a standing ovation as they take a bow on stage with the kitchen staff before music fills the air and the dance floor becomes a jumbled mess of bodies trying their best to keep to the beat of the music. They don't stop dancing until Shana's voice comes over the speakers announcing the time to introduce the Winter King and Queen.

Ryan and Jessie are the winners, and I love how each runner-up is as happy for their win as they would have been for their own.

Each year, the King and Queen get to pick their court, which is usually just the runners-up, but this year, of course, these two drag Storm and I up on the stage too.

The night ends in exhaustion for all and excitement for the festival tomorrow.

In Storm's truck on the way back to the condo complex, I give him the lowdown on tomorrow's activities.

"I'm sure the guys would love to have your help with the snow tube run," I say.

"Snow tube run?" he asks. "What exactly does a snow tube run entail?"

"We have this steep hill at the back of the property. It's an access road to the utility equipment. For the Winter Festival, we give the kids snow tubes, roasting pans, cookie sheets, pretty much anything that can be used as a projectile down a hill on snow and ice. It's really not safe, but..." I shrug. "What's the high premium we pay for insurance for?"

"Sounds like fun," Storm says. "Count me in."

Pulling into the complex, Storm nods at Ace sitting watch, assuring no one without permission has entered the property. It makes me feel safe and scared at the same time. Safe because I know with Ace, Callan or Elliot here on watch, no one will get close, but scared because there's a reason for them to be here in the first place.

"Relax," Storm says, with a hand squeezing my knee. "We haven't seen anything suspicious since the break-in. It might have been a random act and just a coincidence with bad timing. Black talked to that rent-a-cop down at the station, and he said there's been an uptick in crime in the area since the tourism has picked up."

"If you want me to relax, maybe you should take my mind off things," I taunt.

"You know how I feel about a challenge, and that sounds like one to me."

Storm throws the car in park.

"Mmm." I hum. Reaching between his legs, I cup his growing bulge. "Are you sure you're *up* for it?"

Storm growls and pulls me to his face with a grip on the nape of my neck. "Little girl, you're playing with fire."

"Stop, drop, and roll."

Pushing his door open, Storm stomps to my side of the car and flings me over his shoulder, fireman style. "Daddy is going to have to teach you not to play with matches, huh?"

"I like the way they burn."

Storm chuckles as he slams his condo door shut and makes his way to the bedroom.

Placing me on my feet, he wordlessly strips me bare.

"Stand right here," he orders. "Just like this. Don't move. I want to see you. All of you."

He means more than my naked flesh, and I'm not sure I can give him what he asks for.

Reading my mind, he says, "You can. Don't doubt yourself or question the way I make you feel. You make me feel the same."

I pause, breath held for excitement over what was sure to come, and I let him take in his fill.

"Kiss me," I beg.

When Storm holds still, I feel like a bad girl being denied his love and affection. I squeeze my eyes shut to lessen the disappointment and plead to him with his name whined from my lips. "Storm."

His mouth comes down over mine in a hard, heated kiss to silence my complaint, lips damp and cool, firm and strong as he moans and demands my submission. His mouth claims what's his in slow, deep kisses.

Knowing I need to be a good girl if I want this to continue, I force myself, to remain compliant. But with his touch on my skin, I can't help myself and I kiss him back.

"I love the way you melt like a kitten in my hands when I have you by the nape of your neck or your throat," he says, his hands gently squeezing to apply pressure to the spots before his mouth crashes over mine again.

When he squeezes harder still, our eyes lock for long seconds as the world around me blurs into nothing but the sound of Storm's breathing and his scent floating around me.

Finally, he lets go with a gentle slap to my cheek and his voice rough in my ears. "Breathe."

I gasp for much-needed air, then try to speak, but nothing comes out. I want to say the words on the tip of my tongue, but something holds me back. It's certainly not the thrill of excitement sliding up and down my spine when Storm moves to extricate his cock.

I reach for his zipper with a trembling hand pushing his out of the way. I make quick work yanking the zipper down and smile when his hard flesh brushes against my palm. I free his cock reverently and lean in to inhale his masculine scent.

"You're so perfect here," I murmur. "So thick and long with this vein, I love to run my tongue over." I trace it with my fingertip and Storm shivers.

He moans softly, and I gently caress him. His dick pulses and twitches in my hand as my eyes stay focused on him. His cock is perfect, the head large and dark with a ridge he loves me to flick my tongue over. Unable to wait a moment longer, I do just that and can't think of anything softer or smoother.

"Oh, Char." He gasps. When I look up at Storm, his head is thrown back, the muscles of his neck flexed. "I need you." His dick is leaking from the tip as he fists my hair in the grip of his hands and orders me to my knees with a slight shove in that direction. "Open your mouth and suck my cock until I tell you to stop," he demands. "And stop thinking."

I don't hesitate. I lean into him and press my open mouth to his thigh. His hands find their way into my hair to guide my mouth to his tip.

I suck it in between my lips, letting my tongue circle his crown. He fits perfectly, cradled on my tongue. I use it to wet his cock until it slides smoothly in and out of my mouth. The whole time, Storm offers his encouragement and praise for my skills. His hands in my hair, keep me in place, holding me where he wants me, stroking me as he uses my mouth for his pleasure.

I force my mind to clear and concentrate on the feel of Storm sinking deeper into the back of my throat. I stroke and suck, worshiping his cock, as I coax thunderous sounds from him.

Storm growls as he hardens more in my mouth, encouraging me to suck harder.

I hollow my cheeks and suck, taking him in and out with each stroke of my lips and every thrust of his hips.

When he bottoms out, his hips pressed against my face, his cock at the back of my throat, I feel like I'm drowning, but it isn't an unpleasant sensation.

I gag and sputter as he pushes in deeper. My eyes bulge at the prospect I'm not going to be able to hold my breath much longer, but I certainly can't breathe with his girth and length stretching my mouth and filling my airway.

When I finally pull away to catch my breath, he chuckles. "Not so fast. Daddy is going to put that burning fire in your throat out. Make me come."

I gasp, a quick inhale of air, then open for him again and take him easily to the back of my throat, devouring his taste and absorbing his touch.

Storm growls. "Oh, god! Fuck, I'm so close."

His skin is damp where my hands rest on his thighs and my forehead brushes his abdomen. He strokes the top of my hair and says, "Who's Daddy's good girl? Jesus, Char, you're so fucking good at this."

I let my fingertips explore his hard planes and a low, guttural moan slips from his lips at the caress.

"The minute I come, I want you naked on your back with your legs wide open for me. I'm going to go down on you until my dick is hard again, then I'm going to flip you to your knees and fuck you. Do I need to tell you where I'm going to have my cock buried?"

I shiver, wanting to both experience that with him and scared it's going to hurt like hell because Storm is not a small man by any means.

"I—I shouldn't let you do that," I say, his dick in my fist. "Good girls don't do that."

"Then there's no problem, Spunky. We already know how bad you are. Now, put my cock back in your mouth so I can come."

"I shouldn't do that either. Good girls don't give blow jobs, and they definitely don't swallow."

"Don't tell me what you should do," he roars, then takes his cock from my fist and jerks himself with the command, "Open those fucking lips and stick out your tongue."

I feel the need building in him, every muscle in his body taut. Then he gasps, his body relaxing into the pleasure as his climax takes hold.

As I obey, Storm throws his head back and releases himself on my tongue. A stream hits my right cheek before he plunges himself back into my open mouth and rides out the rest of his orgasm in my throat.

Arousal surges at my core, and I melt against him.

Storm kisses along my jawline, his tongue leaving a cool, wet path as he goes on an expedition down my neck, only briefly stopping to nibble at the spot where it meets my shoulder before kissing me.

When he tastes himself on my tongue, the sound from him is feral, and it ignites the fire inside me.

He spreads my legs with a tight grip on each thigh and runs his tongue across my collar bone, down to my pebbled nipples. He groans as he takes one in between his lips and rears back, letting it out with a pop and a pinch. He alternates nipples, licking and sucking them until I see stars.

Urgency grows deep in my belly as Storm slides down my body, stopping midway to swirl his tongue around, then dip inside my belly button. I groan and his shaft strains against my leg. My breath catches in my throat.

His hands stroke my body from my face to my toes, spending extended time on my bare shoulder, which has become his favorite location for his mouth. Well, other than where he's heading.

He strokes a hardened nipple with the pad of his thumb, then cups my breasts in his hands before trailing his fingers down my ribs to my hips. "Are you wet, baby?"

"Yes," I moan. "For you, I'm always wet."

His fingers slip inside my pussy, and I nuzzle into his neck, moaning his name and raising my hips in a plea for more attention.

I grasp him. "You're hard already."

He echoes my words. "For you, I'm always hard."

His fingers spread the delicate folds of my pussy, and I moan low in my throat from the need building deep inside.

I palm his heavy erection in my hand and begin to tug, stroking the velvety soft tip, swirling a fingernail around the velvety head.

"I want to be inside you," he whispers. "Right here." His finger rims my tight entrance, and I shiver.

"I know, baby. I know you're scared. I'll go slow. I'm going to make it good, you know that."

I nod. "Yes. I want it, too. I want you there."

"Where, Charlie? Tell me where you want me to bury my thick cock."

"In my ass," I say as naturally as if I was asking him to hold my hand.

Storm lowers his mouth to my core, and the stars I just saw explode into fireworks as the roughness of his scruff blends with the coarseness of his tongue. When he moans and the sound vibrates through me, I cry out.

I'm so close, but I know I can't come unless it's what he wants, so I beg. "Please, Storm. Storm, please, I need to come."

Looking up at me from between my legs with a wicked smirk, he tugs at my clit with his lips and shakes his head.

I arch off the mattress with a howl, much like one of the animals I'm always petrified to encounter on the trail. "Oh, god. I'm coming, I can't stop."

Storm smirks then covers my pussy with his open lips as I climax so hard those stars turned fireworks now take my vision away all together.

"Perfect," Storm says. "Now I'm going to need you on your knees for your spanking for that. Conveniently, you'll be exactly how I need you so I can then fuck that red ass."

Grabbing and flipping me to all fours, Storm readjusts so he's on his knees behind me, then stretches for the bedside table and opens the top drawer where he keeps a few toys. Tonight, he pulls out a paddle I haven't seen before. It looks like firm plywood, a ping–pong variety with the rubber removed, sanded, and varnished to a deep sheen. He swooshes it through the air, then taps it on his palm. "This is going to sting that ass, my naughty girl."

I know protesting is futile, so I brace myself with my hands white knuckling the bed.

"Hands at your sides, young lady," Storm demands. "Or we can tie them back here." His finger runs down each bump of my vertebrate until they stop in the dip of my back.

Then the paddle goes up into the air, whooshes through it, and lands with a firm thwack on its mark, my bare ass. I croak, "One, Daddy."

His subsequent swats are firm enough to elicit yelps, squeaks, and ouches with each pass of the paddle, while I force myself to remember to count each.

I buck my hips from time to time but do my best to keep still to earn his praise. It's only when I remain calm and in place does Storm call me his good girl or tell me how perfect I look on my knees, accepting his punishment with my ass reddened and in the air.

I live for his praise, but I can rapidly feel my ass cheeks changing from hot pink to bright red and staying immobile is growing more challenging, as is counting each swat.

My voice reaches a higher pitch with each pass and by the time I scream ten, I barely recognize my voice.

Five more crisp smacks echo around the room, each packing a wallop as Storm keeps his rhythm until the very end when he hears my throaty howl at number fifteen.

I emit a clear gasp after it and struggle as it becomes increasingly difficult to hang on as he finishes my punishment.

Then I feel our bodies press together, his front to my back. The contact is welcome and hated at the same time. Wanted because I love the closeness of him, hated because my ass is on fire after that spanking and the bristles of his leg hairs annoy my sore skin.

"I'm going to get you nice and ready first," he promises. "I'm going to finger you, then use your natural lube on your ass. I'll use this..." He flips the cap on the lube. "On my dick. All you need to worry about is trusting me enough to relax so you can let me in. That and feeling good, okay?"

"I'll try."

"That's my good girl."

His finger enters me, and I sigh when he crooks it and explores my inner walls. "Just going to make sure you're on the edge."

I moan. Being on the edge sucks compared to going over, but I'm not the experienced one here, so I go with the flow.

"You're so wet, baby. This is going to feel so good for both of us. This pussy is going to keep us nice and slippery."

Removing his finger, Storm circles it around my ass's entrance, and I groan at how good it already feels.

"Like that, little girl?"

"Yes, Daddy."

He pushes in a second finger. "Just need to open you up a little, then we'll get started with me."

Storm spreads his fingers, scissoring them, then fucking me with them. It's a maddening pattern and if keeping me on edge is where he wants me, I'm there triple fold.

"I'm ready," I state. "Please. Do it. I want you."

Crack.

He spanks my ass. "Who is in charge when we fuck?"

Sucking in a gulp at the second slap, I say, "You, Daddy. Sorry."

"Damn fucking right. Now lift that ass up a little for me. Cheek on the bed, arch your back."

I try my best to get into the position he asks and when he moans and calls me his good girl, I know I've at least come close to the mark.

"Just going to lube my dick, then you're going to do everything I say exactly how I tell you to, so I don't hurt you, understand?"

I nod and get another handful of slaps and spanks for not using my words like I know I'm supposed to.

"Sorry again, Daddy. I'm excited. Not thinking. Scared."

His hand runs the length of my back then the other joins and he repositions my hips, pulling them up before pushing down on my back to make me arch perfectly.

"Stay just like this. Your asshole is so tight."

A plop of his saliva lands directly on my tight hole, then Storm groans and strokes the lube up and down his shaft.

"I'm going to need you to heave in a big gulp of air and hold it until I tell you to let it out. When you do, you're going to bear down, right here." His finger enters my ass again to the knuckle and swirls around. He grunts. "So fucking tight. I'm not going to last long in here."

"Oh, god!" I cry out when I feel the blunt tip of his head gently pressing into my entrance.

"You're okay. Going to make this so fucking good for you. Ready?"

"I don't..." Storm presses in a smidge more. "Yes. Yes, I'm ready."

"Heave in a big breath and hold it until I say to let go. Then you're going to bear down and let it out, okay?"

"Storm, yes. Just do it. Please. Now."

"Take in a breath," he demands, and his hips twitch. "Fuck! Let go and bear down. Let me in."

I do as he says, and I feel the head of his cock slide in to the ridge I love to run my tongue around.

But as fast as I feel him there, he's gone.

"Ahhh..."

Storm grunts and swears, then pushes back into me, giving me more than he did a second ago.

And so it goes for thrust after thrust until his body presses flush to mine, his cock completely encased inside me.

"Oh, fuck! You're so hot and tight in this ass, baby. When I start fucking you, it's going to go fast because I'm going to blow my load in this ass so fucking quick."

"Do it. Fuck me, Storm, fuck me now."

"Call me Daddy."

"Fuck me now, Daddy."

"Shit!"

Storm thrusts with grunts and curses as he finds a pace he likes, then he checks in with me. "You okay? Doing so good. Proud of you. Feel good?"

I can't keep up with his questions, so I nod even though I know he wants words.

"My god, I need you to go off now, baby. I'm about to come in your ass."

He shifts his hips and gains deeper entry inside the place only he's ever been.

I look back over a shoulder into his magnificently gorgeous face, rugged but with delicate eyes only for me.

With hips gyrating, Storm pulls out then guides his engorged cock back in so swiftly and smoothly, I know this isn't wrong. It's too perfect to be. It feels too good not to be right and the feeling just keeps climbing closer and closer to perfection.

Nothing could have prepared me for this sensation of complete and utter fullness, not his fingers or any toy. Only his cock could be this perfect.

Storm's thumb finds my clit and strums as he plows into me with such force, the only way I haven't gone through the wall is because of the punishing grip he has on my hips.

His fingers are going to leave a mark.

"Come with me, Charlie. Right fucking now while I fill this ass."

"Fuck!"

"Tell me where you want Daddy to come."

"Come in my ass, Daddy, please. Oh, god! I'm coming."

I look over my shoulder to stare into his face.

His breath comes in short, raspy pants matching mine as he stares at the spot where we connect.

The sight has me straining toward my orgasm beginning to tremble through me.

Shifting, I grind my ass against him, and that is all it takes for us both to lose control.

I scream out my climax, and Storm leans over me and pulls my mouth to his. As I whimper into his kiss, he roars, and unloads hot, wet spurt after spurt into me.

Then all I feel is wetness. So much wetness and slick slides of his cock through my sensitive flesh as his fingers enter my pussy and his cock continues to fuck my ass as he rides his orgasm to the very end.

My climax is never-ending. I spiral higher and higher as Storm tenses inside me. His gasps turn to moans in my ear. "You made me come in your ass, you bad girl."

Slap.

"Storm."

"I know, Char. I know, baby. I'm right there with you."

I don't know what to think, I only know how I feel.

I love Storm.

He gives me everything I've always wanted.

Love.

Everything I've been seeking.

Peace.

Everything I need.

Belonging.

Finally admitting it to myself, a lightness spreads in my heart that's never been there before. When he repositions us, I cling to his body as our lips meet. Feeling his thick, exquisite cock swell against my belly, I murmur against his mouth, begging for him to enter me.

Wanting him.

Needing him.

He reaches for the wipes he keeps to clean up, then he slides quickly and smoothly into my warm wetness, undulating against me, our bodies wrapped around each other.

As Storm moves to exit me, I let it all go.

In the next second, I find myself sprawled across Storm's body, pressing into his flat, muscular abdomen.

Cradled in Storm's arms, fear and uncertainty fade away as our bodies mold together, and he slips deeper inside me. My lungs swell with desire to finally say those words on the tip of my tongue. "Storm," I say, my eyes locked to his. "I—I'm falling in love with you."

"I need to take care of you, but first..." He pulls my lips to his with his hands on the sides of my face. "I'm glad to hear that." He kisses my forehead. "I already did my falling. I'm completely wrecked by you."

I smile. At least I think I do, but who really knows? Because my body feels so loose and my mind floats through space as I look into his face and see my desires and emotions mirrored in his expression.

I must doze off because I remotely remember hearing him mumble something about how perfect I am and being right back. Then, while I still feel him inside me, he's there cleaning me with a gentle hand.

I'm going to be sore in the best way tomorrow for the Winter Festival, and I fall asleep with a smile on my face at the thought of having the reminder of what we just did with me all day when I'm Miss Tyler and in charge.

Storm

I wake my girl with my tongue, lapping at all her sorest spots until she shifts her hands into my hair and comes in my mouth. Then I gently carry her into the shower and soap her up.

She reaches for my erection, straining for her, but I push her hand away. "You're way too sore after last night. You still feel me here?" I ask with my hand, brushing her ass.

She nods and bites her bottom lip.

"How about here?" I cup her pussy in my palm.

"Yes. Everywhere, Storm, but I want more. I'm sore in a good way."

"I know you think you are, but what we did last night is enough for a couple days."

"A couple days?"

I laugh at her expression, then succumb to her evil plans as she sinks onto the seat in the shower and grasps my cock at the base.

I take her mouth gently and come inside it before the water gets cold.

Finally dressed, we make our way into my kitchen, and I go for the coffee maker while Charlie takes out bread and eggs.

I meet her at the stovetop with our coffees in hand. Handing hers over, I grab some bacon and pop it into the microwave.

We eat together as we have each morning since she moved in with me and the domesticity has the opposite effect on me as I thought it would.

I'm done playing games and today, after the festival, I'm calling Mac and telling him there is no way Charlie is involved in anything illegal. I'm then calling my brother and letting him know he'll have a winter wonderland he can bring Lainey and the kids to, because tomorrow, I'm starting my search for a house.

I'm not leaving Lime Peak or Charlie...ever.

At the camp, I'm greeted by the guys with hearty pats to my back and huge smiles when they see I'm not alone. Callan, Ace, and Elliot came to help with the snow tube run that is apparently the bane of their existence each year.

"I've never been happier I was dragged into this," Brad says as he eyes my muscular friends.

Rourke laughs. "With their muscles, I can't fault you and honestly, the help is welcomed, so enjoy the eye candy."

Ian rolls his eyes. "I have muscles, too, you know, and I've been here helping every year."

Brad and Rourke laugh together.

"It's cute that you think it's the same," Rourke says to his brother as Brad's jaw drops when Elliot takes off his coat to get to work shoveling the paths and making the slopes and slides.

A few of the older boys, including Nicky Gillespie and his motley crew, offer to help.

They're at the age where they're dying to fly down the run on a cookie sheet but feel stupid for wanting to, so they feign indifference and offer their budding muscles up. Not being stupid men, we happily accept.

It doesn't take long for the boys to become as enamored with Callan, Ace, and Elliot as they are with me, and they ask us questions about the military, seeing action, and, of course, girls.

We spend a few hours doing our best to make each of the runs as safe as possible, while still offering a thrill. Each is its own level of fun, from mild to terrifying—if you hit the curve just right on that one, you'll soar into the air before landing in a snow pile.

By the time we're done, and the others have the food booths and craft tables set up, the vendors arrive and set up their goods.

Then, it's just the families and people from the community we're waiting for when I turn to my friends and say, "I'm calling Mac tonight. She's not into anything illegal, and I'm telling her everything."

Callan smirks at Ace, and Elliot runs a hand through his hair.

"What's that look?"

"Look?" Callan asks in a rehearsed voice. "What look?"

"What's he up to?" I ask Ace.

"You really don't want to know. Just leave it."

"No. Tell me what's going on. If this has something to do with Charlie—"

Elliot jumps into our back and forth. "Black is an idiot. We all know this. I warned them this was ridiculous, but here we are. Once again, no one can listen to me."

"You yelled something about this through the bathroom door while you fucked your wife bent over the toilet seat."

I stare at Ace for clarification. He explains that Elliot and his wife Courtney, who he still calls by the fake name she gave him when they first met, have a kink about having sex in bathrooms. Apparently, it's where they first did it and it just sort of became a thing. Not one to judge people for what gets them off, I smile at the picture it creates in my mind.

Staring Ace down, I ask again, "What the fuck is Black up to?"

Sighing, Ace says, "The crazy, no social skills sap decided that you were lonely like he was before he met Jordan. He's known Charlie since they were kids and apparently, she was sweet to him when others did nothing but make fun of him. He was weirder than he is even now, so it's easy to believe. When Monti and I met him, he was a total whack job. Anyway, Charlie has been unlucky in love for a while, dating assholes and talking about using dating apps where Black was convinced a creeper was going to find and kill her."

"Hey!" Elliot scoffs. "Adams and I joined a dating app and were matched together. Look at us now."

I fling my head back. "Stone's app?" I ask. "Compatible Companions that matches sexually like-minded people for kink?"

"And relationships. Obviously," Elliot defends.

"Obviously. But what does this have to do with Charlie and me?" Even as I say the words, I know the answer. "Fuck! Seriously? Black!"

"What?" Callan asks. "Jordan said I needed to stop being so egocentric and start thinking about the way others are feeling. I truly don't give a flying fuck what most people are feeling, but I love Charlie, and you're a decent guy."

He states this as if it's enough of an explanation and should make perfect sense to everyone. It only does in his neurodivergent mind.

I run a hand over the beanie on the top of my head. "So, you set this all up? There's never been a concern she was involved in smuggling drugs? Mac went along with this?"

Ace lets out a hearty laugh from the pit of his belly. "Yeah, that was fun to watch. Black had a PowerPoint and everything. It included how many more years your dick was going to work and when Charlie's eggs were going to expire. It was so good."

I stare at Callan like he's as batshit crazy as he is.

"I can show it to you," he offers.

"Nah, I'm good. And my dick is fine and not dying anytime soon."

"Research shows—" Callan starts, but shuts up when I hold up a hand and Elliot yanks him back a step or two.

"The drug thing is bogus, but the identify theft is real, and as far as we can tell, so was the break-in."

"Okay, well then, let's keep our energy there. I'm keeping her at my place until I figure out what I'm doing."

Elliot lifts a brow. "What are you doing? You moving here, Roland?"

"Well, I'm not leaving her, so I guess I might be."

I don't see my girl for the next couple of hours other than in passing as she stops by the snow tube run with a coffee for me or an apple cider donut. She holds my hand and stretches up on her toes when she brings me treats and gives my lips a sweet brush of hers.

I don't love the increasing number of people at the festival and the only thing keeping me from losing my motherfucking mind over her safety are the cameras the guys installed around campus weeks ago that I have cued up on an app on my phone. Well, that and the fact that with her parents not being here and her sister running late, Jessie hasn't left Charlie's side all day. The little angel brings me a treat of her own each time Charlie stops by to pay me a visit.

I think the pair of them are trying to fatten me up.

Everyone has a great time, from what I can tell, and when the end of the day nears, the guys and I are all ready for some inside time with our feet up and a rest for our biceps. Shoveling snow is no joke of a workout.

A young woman approaches and by her description, I'd bet she's Jessie's sister who works at the camp during their vacation weeks and summers.

"Hi." She introduces herself with a friendly handshake. "I'm Montana, one of the teachers for next week. My sister actually attends here, too. I'm looking for her. Her name is

Jessie. The snow tube run is always her favorite and I'm guessing you're Storm."

"Oh!" My face breaks into a smile and beams over my fondness for the young girl. "Your sister never stops talking about you. Well, when she's not talking about Ryan."

Montana laughs, and I confirm I'm who she assumed.

"Yeah, she talks about you and Charlie all the time, too. That's why I came over to ask you. Not many other guys working around here that fit the description she gave me."

"I'm afraid to ask." I chuckle.

"Like the puffy, green guy from that scary ride we went on, only he's not scary or green. He's cream color and really nice."

I laugh louder. "The Hulk?"

"Yup. I see you speak Jessie already."

"She's a great girl," I say as my blood runs cold when the sound of child laughter is replaced by the shrill of an alarm. I frantically turn to the guys and demand, "Where?"

Callan already has his phone in hand with the app cued up. "Admin building."

"Fuck!" I curse. The admin building is the farthest from where we are.

We take off running none the less, without explanation for Montana, who tries to keep up for a second then gives up.

My heart thuds in my chest as Ace, Callan, Elliot, and I approach the center of the campus and split up to cover more ground, in case someone is trying to find an escape route. Whichever way they go, they'll have to pass one of us.

I can kick myself for the false feeling of security this magical place gave me. I let my guard down when I should have been acting overzealously with Charlie's safety. I should have demanded she stayed by my side at the snow tube run, or I should have tailed her everywhere she moved.

Now I'm paying the price for giving her the freedom she demanded.

If this ends in our favor, I won't make that mistake again. Charlene Tyler will never leave my sight for as long as I live.

My heart stutters in my chest when another alarm blares through the air, then the sound of tires on ice and gravel meets my ears.

A black truck, sleek and intentionally missing plates, barrels at a group of teens on the path ahead of me.

I yell to Nicky, but not all of his crew moves as fast as the agile athlete, and my body slams the slowest movers to the side of the path in the nick of time.

Sitting up, I pull my piece to fire at the tires of the vehicle. Unfortunately, without a safe enough shot—there were too many kids and parents gathered around—I miss my chance and the truck disappears as I call Black and scream into my phone. "There's a black truck barreling through campus. They just almost killed a path full of kids. I couldn't get a shot off safe enough."

Is this another coincidence or is the truck here to bring danger to Charlie?

I don't have the time to think about either and I also don't bother to address the scared students and families as they watch me run in the direction of the admin building with my gun at the ready.

Panic soars through my blood when the building comes into view, Callan, Ace, and Elliot arriving at the same time from their paths.

We dash into the building, weapons blazing, but the silence tells me it's too late. Whoever was here and set off the alarm is gone. I'm just hoping when they left, they were alone, and Charlie is somewhere else on campus.

Callan's uncharacteristic touch on my shoulder tells me that's not the case. He hands me his phone with the video from a handful of minutes ago cued up.

The less than five minutes of footage I watch are some of the worst minutes of my life.

On screen, three masked intruders with weapons only seen in the world of illegal firearms come into view seconds before I see Charlie and Jessie run through the main office into the lobby, where they run smack into one of the masked men. Seconds later, he raises a gun at the camera and all goes black.

I have no idea who the men are or why they took Charlie and Jessie—my two options are they're the same men who stole Charlie's identity and think she has their stolen money, or it was someone from my past here to seek revenge. Neither option is good.

"We need to check the building to be sure they're not here, then we'll do the grounds."

"Fuck!" I shout and bang my fist on Anita's desk. "We need more hands."

"On it," Elliot says with his phone already to his ear. "Dad—"

I don't hear the conversation with his father, a retired Special Agent, but I know if he's calling him, his father-in-law, Rick Roman, will be in tow. The two are tight with Mac, so I'm sure my boss will be in the know before I have the chance to explain any of what has happened since I arrived in Lime Peak.

"We need to get moving," Ace states. "We're losing time."

"If they have Jessie, we need to let her family know."

"Her sister is here. She's working as a teacher at the camp next week. I was talking to her when the alarm sounded."

Not having time to worry about finding and getting Montana Webber up to speed, we comb through the spaces of the main office, Charlie's private quarters, and the rest of the administrators' spaces.

When I hear the faint sounds of a female cry, my heart finally beats again, and I fly through Rourke's office door and follow the sound to his closet.

Flinging it open, I waste no time in reaching for Charlie.

But it's not Charlie I find trembling in the closet's corner with her tear-stained face in her tiny hands.

Jessie.

I take the scared girl into my arms and carry her out of her hiding spot in the dark. "Jessie, are you okay?"

"Where's Miss T?"

"I don't know, baby. Did you see someone with a mask?"

She nods, and I place her on Rourke's sofa at the same time the door flies open and her sister falls at her feet.

"What's going on?" Montana asks through gasping breaths as she drags her sister's body into her arms. "Are you okay? You're shaking."

"The bad men took Miss T. They had masks and guns and called her bad names I'm not allowed to say. She told me to run and hide."

Montana's questioning eyes meet mine. "What is she talking about?"

I sigh. "I don't have all the details, and understand, others I can't share, but what I can say and what I do know is someone stole Charlie's identity and used her name to steal money. I think they may have come looking for it and taken her."

"Are you fucking serious?" Montana asks.

"That's one of the bad words then men said a lot to Miss T."

My blood boils.

Did they use the word as a verb and threaten to fuck her? Because taking her from me is enough for them to have to die. Harming her in any way, especially sexually, will earn them a very painful and slow coming death.

I'm pacing the floor minutes later when Ace comes in, a smile brightening his face when he sees Jessie is safe in her sister's arms.

"They left her?"

"Yeah, but Jessie confirmed they took Charlie. All I can get from her is they said fuck a lot."

Our eyes meet, and I know we're thinking the same thing.

"Motherfuckers better keep their hands to themselves."

"Yeah." It's all I can say past the lump in my throat.

"Charlie's office is destroyed. They were definitely looking for something I don't think they found."

"If they think she has their money or whatever else they're after, she doesn't. When they figure that out, she becomes useless to them."

"Rick, Dave, and Mac are all en route. The King brothers have a connection through their dad with the bureau, so they're working that end with border patrol."

"Fuck, I hadn't thought of—"

"Yeah, if Bridget was abducted, man, I wouldn't be thinking either. We got you," Ace says.

I nod and exit Rourke's office to see the damage in Charlie's and to be anywhere that might make me feel her again.

I can't feel her in the air in Rourke's space, but maybe I can in hers and she'll send me a message through the strong connection we have.

I pace through her office, careful as I can be not to step on anything. Callan hasn't had the time to process the scene yet, and I don't want to disturb something that might give the brainiac a clue who the men are and where they took my girl.

I plop myself down on the floor and watch the video footage for the millionth time while wanting to do nothing more than kill one of the motherfuckers. I'm finally in a space silent enough that I'm able to hear the audio.

Jessie was right. They said fuck a lot.

Unfortunately, I was right, too, and the word was a verb coming from their mouths.

The sick fucks threatened to share Jessie after using slurs to describe her disability.

My heart dropped to my feet when Charlie said, "Leave her alone. I'll do whatever you want, and I won't fight you. She's an innocent child that has no experience. I know what you want."

Jesus fuck, Charlie offered herself to them on a silver platter to save Jessie from the gang rape they taunted her with.

It makes me so proud of her while I want to slap her ass red for what she did.

I also want to kill those motherfuckers for putting her in the situation. If one of them even touched a single hair on my girl's head, they'll spend their last minutes before they arrive in hell regretting it.

Finding a sweater on the back of her chair as I rise again to pace, I bring it to my face and inhale Charlie's familiar scent.

It nearly brings me to my knees. Needing to keep it together for the best chance of finding Charlie, I fight the urge to further destroy her office.

"You okay?" I hear Elliot ask.

I groan out a male grunt. "I don't know what to do."

"I know, bud, but you gotta try to keep your shit together. For her, okay?"

"I know. I'm trying."

"My dad is about an hour away. Rick and Mac are with him. We'll find her."

I slam my fist into the closest wall, then run it through my hair. "Not fast enough," I seethe.

Elliot doesn't try to tell me to calm down or placate me. He knows damn well if his wife was missing and all evidence pointed to horny men with less than stellar morals, he'd be as ready to kill one of the motherfuckers as I am right now. "Let's try to piece this together as best we can while we wait for the others."

"Thanks," I say and accept the bottle of water he must have been holding in his hand for a bit. "Where's Black? Maybe he found their whereabouts or who the fuck they are by now."

I can't stomach not knowing where Charlie is and what they're doing to her. I know she appears as the tough in charge principal to her families, students, and staff, but that mask was wearing her out and when with me, she removed it to relax and let me take over. She isn't trained or mentally equipped to be held captive. What if they hurt her beyond repair?

I never told her the truth about why I came to Lime Peak.

I meant to. I was just waiting for the right time because I knew she was going to be mad I'd lied to her. Maybe not upon arrival. She'd understand I was sent to do a job, even if it was bogus, but after all this time, she'll be mad I never came clean.

Now, she may never know that even before I found out the entire case was a ruse devised by Callan and Mac to set Charlie and me up, I didn't believe she was into anything illegal. If she had been, I'm not sure I wouldn't have made excuses for her, so we could still have been together.

Yeah, turning a blind eye to illegal activities so I could make her mine is how bad I have it for Charlie Tyler.

And now she may never know because I might lose her forever.

"If this was revenge on you, the assholes would have made sure you knew it was them. They would be all over the place boasting about it, right? So that's probably good news."

I scoff as Ace sidles up next to us, Callan only a few steps away, with his nose buried in his phone. "Yeah, so some unknown assholes have her. That's so much better."

A hand on my shoulder has me turning to see Charlie's staff rushing through the door.

"What the fuck is going on?" Rourke demands. "Where's Charlie?"

"We don't know," Elliot states to save me from admitting that I failed to keep her safe.

"What do you mean, you don't know?" Kayley asks. "Did something bad happen? Did she leave?"

I shake my head. "We're not sure of all the details yet, but it might have something to do with the identity theft."

"The identity theft?" Anita inquires with a concerned hand going to her chest and another tugging her coat closed as if she's cold inside the heated building. "You don't think she was involved in that, do you? Because I can tell you..." She gets right in my face for the last part of her sentence. "Charlene Tyler is not a thief."

"I know," I say, sounding every bit embarrassed as I am for ever thinking she was. "I know. I lied to you about who I am and why I came to Lime Peak."

"Man," Ace says in warning. He, Black, and Elliot understandably don't want their cover shot to shit, even though I'm pretty sure everyone in Falls Village, Lime Peak, and Waterland Isle already suspects they are who they are and do what they do.

I clear my throat, but Callan steps in and says, "Enough. We know you're not that clueless. We keep our noses down and don't cause trouble, so you overlook the fact that we have more money than our cover jobs allow."

"Black," Ace warns, but Callan ignores him.

"Charlie and I have known each other since we were kids. I attended Camp SubLime when I was an angry, confused teenager, and she was nice to me. Her father was the first male figure who treated me like a human being. I stayed in touch with him. When I had the means, I began offering the camp my financial support. When I moved to Falls Village, I joined the board. I watched Charlie looking for love in all the wrong type of men. Like my wife, she's a strong woman with a take-charge leadership job, but that's not what she wants or needs in a relationship."

I hear a familiar voice chime in behind me and I turn to see Mac. "Storm Roland thought he was happy with the young girls rotating through his bed because he doesn't think he deserves anything more. Black and I were sick of watching it."

"You were in on this with him?" Ace asks. "We're totally fucked if he's got you thinking his schemes are good ideas."

Mac chuckles. "He got to Drea. My wife forced my hand at the romance. And yes, after that, I helped Black get Storm here to meet Charlie. After the initial meeting, their connection was on them."

"It was instant," I admit. "The minute I saw her file, I was a goner. I think she felt the same about me the minute I plowed into her on the trail."

Mac raises a curious eyebrow as Dave and Rick approach me to offer their extended hands.

"We've got news," Dave says. "We're going to need you to sit down and let us talk, but we need to do that in private."

I make eye contact around the room with each of Charlie's friends, silently asking them to trust me.

With collective nods all around, I watch as Rourke leads the group of Charlie's loyal friends out of her office and I collapse, sliding down the wall, onto the floor. "Tell me what you know," I demand, as I sink my head into my hands.

"We know who has her. Bragging on the dark web, Black has tabs on them. They know who you are and the tie you have with her."

I don't know if I should be relieved we have eyes on her or terrified the assholes who took Charlie know she's connected to me. What I do know is Charlie is gone and because she holds my heart in her hand, I'm not going to survive without her.

Charlie

I wake, groggy and confused. Things make less sense when I look around at my surroundings until I remember what happened.

Jessie and I were in the admin building because she started her period and walking back to her dorm would have taken longer than coming to my office. I have the supplies she needs in my private bathroom, so it made sense.

On our way out, we heard male voices.

At first, I figured it was Rourke and Brad, or maybe Ian, Storm even, looking for me. I never expected to run into men with ski masks on their faces and guns in their hands. When we did, I instantly knew it wasn't good.

The alarm blaring was another sign, but that took a while to register. We don't have an alarm system that sounds like the one that blared so loud, the whole town of Lime Peak must have been able to hear it.

When the realization of who these masked men were and what they wanted hit, I knew I had to do whatever I could to keep Jessie calm and safe.

When they used that awful slur in front of her, I felt her cringe through our connected hands. Thankfully, she knew their language was inappropriate and not words she was allowed to use, but as scared and confused as she was, she also, thankfully, wasn't understanding their meaning.

But I was.

When the words, "...I'll do whatever you want, and I won't fight you..." came out of my mouth, I knew I had boxed myself into a corner. Knowing what it meant to care for someone so much you'd sacrifice yourself to keep them safe finally made sense.

But as I come to my senses now, my clothes are on and in place. Not a hair on my head has been harmed or touched.

Were the men just trying to scare me? Maybe they were underlings and decided better against doing something that wasn't part of their boss's strict orders. Maybe they found their consciences before gang raping me like they threatened to do to Jessie. Whatever the reason, I'm certain no one has touched me as I sit up on the bed in a hotel room.

Hmmm. A pretty damn nice hotel room, not some shithole on the side of a highway.

Nothing is making much sense, but I'm free to roam around, so I stand on shaky legs and stretch.

They must have drugged me to sleep, so I've no idea how much time has passed since they took me from campus nor do I know where I am, but I say a little prayer that Storm knows I'm gone and can figure out a way to find me. I say an even bigger one that Jessie is safe and sound on campus and Montana has arrived by now to be with her.

Looking around to explore my surroundings before stupidly trying to make a break for it, I hear male voices in another room. I'm in a suite's bedroom, and the voices must be coming from my captors, who are holding court out in the main room.

I hear a toilet flush, then male laughter before someone calls the other a fucking pussy and laughs again.

Hoping to maybe find out my whereabouts, I move closer to the door where the voices are coming from and settle myself on the plush carpet.

"I still can't believe the fucking luck of this shit, man," a deep voice says.

A male chuckle is followed by, "Storm motherfucking Roland and his band of brothers."

"I know," another quips. "The coincidence of this is too fucking much. But it was perfect. Roland led us right to Tyler."

"What I still think is suspicious is Black believing she's a drug smuggler. I get Roland taking the job to take Tyler down, but how did Black not know she wasn't corrupt?"

Callan thinks I'm smuggling drugs? I can't be hearing things correctly. Maybe I'm more drugged than I thought, or dreaming, because he's my friend. Callan and I have known each other for years. He'd never think I was smuggling drugs.

I try my best to silence my thoughts so I can hear more of their conversation.

After sitting and quietly listening for a good thirty minutes, I'm more confused than before, but that emotion has taken the back burner to down and out pissed.

Fury fills my veins as I process the men's conversation.

Storm Roland owns a financial planning and money management firm with offices in New York and London. Since semi-retiring, he's opened a branch in Westchester to be close to his twin brother and his family.

None of that was a shock. Storm and I spoke a little about his career and his brother, Corey, who is married to his college sweetheart and has two teenage kids.

I also made the connection between him, Callan, Ace, and Elliot, so I knew Storm had some military affiliation.

Callan, Ace, and Elliot like to think the residents of Falls Village, Lime Peak, and Waterland Isle don't know they do something undercover for the military or some private firm. My best guess is they are all ex-military, working for a private agency that's off the grid. Knowing Callan for as long as I have, going rogue would make sense for him. And whatever he's up to, so are Ace Lyons and Elliot Montgomery. Obviously, Storm is as well.

But it's the next thing I hear that has my blood boiling. Storm only came to Lime Peak because he accepted the job of taking down the drug smuggling principal at a camp for children with special needs.

Want to guess who that is?

Mmm.

And apparently, he was doing a bang-up job by banging the suspect...i.e. me.

So I piece together what's going on—Storm, Callan, Ace, and Elliot work undercover for someone named Mac. Mac hired Storm to investigate me for drug smuggling. My identity was stolen by the men who are my kidnappers, and apparently archenemies with Storm and the guys he works with. The entire time with Storm has been a lie—I feel more like a fool with each passing second.

I thought I finally found the one, my match, in Storm. He made me feel safe enough to admit I needed to submit in bed to feel sexual fulfillment. He made sex fun. He let me play with my Daddy kink and never judged me. He likes it, too, but not in a strange way. Sure, he makes me call him Daddy when he smacks my ass or when he's holding my orgasm at bay, but we both know it's being shared between us in a safe and consensual way. He would never belittle me in public or make me call him that in front of my friends.

Storm is all male, a sexually dominant man who likes control, but he's respectful of my feelings and genuinely seems to want me to explore every side of myself until I figure out exactly what it is I need to feel secure in my identity as a professional woman and a woman in a man's bed.

I've always seen those personas as separate. Storm was making me believe they could be the same.

But now I don't know what to think.

Was it all a lie?

Was everything between us pretend, a means to an end for him?

Did he give me what he knew I needed to feel safe enough to let my guard down with him so he could easily and quickly slip into my life, only to investigate me?

It feels like hours later when I still don't have the answer to any of those questions, but a commotion has me startling out of my thoughts.

Then I hear the voice of the man I thought I loved, but now wasn't even sure who he was.

There's male yelling then grunting as a fight must begin between, I'm guessing, Storm, Callan and the guys with the men who took me from campus.

I wonder how they found me, but before I have time to think about the answer, the door flies open and chaos fills my vision.

Then, through yelling and fists flying, I see Storm's body airborne as he jumps in my direction, and the air pops with a loud crack of thunder.

Then everything in me goes black as his enormous body crashes down on mine.

Storm was shot jumping in front of a bullet for me.

Storm

I found the woman of my dreams, the one I'm convinced is my soulmate, on a trail here in Lime Peak, Maine, by crashing into her. Now, here I am, taking her to the ground with my body again. Only this time, it's to save her life by possibly giving away mine.

I happily do it. My only regret is if I don't make it long enough to explain everything to her, she might not believe how I really felt from Callan and the guys.

"Umph," Charlie groans into my ear as her tiny body wiggles under me, then she screams my name and pushes at my body.

Knowing I'm probably squishing her, but keeping her blocked with my body, I refuse to move.

"Storm," she cries again and again. "Storm, are you okay?"

I've been shot before. Shot enough times, actually, to know that even when shock is setting in, there's pain and right now, I'm not feeling any. So, I'm either really dying and numb to it, or the bullet didn't hit me.

"Shh," I say to calm her down and to keep her quiet. I don't know who is still firing shots, and I need her to stay still and under me if I'm going to get her out of here unharmed.

"Storm, you took a bullet for me. You need help."

Callan's chuckle fills my ears, and I realize the room has grown silent other than his laughter. "Nah, the guy's aim was for shit. The bullet's in the wall about a yard from him."

I brush her hair out of her face, off her forehead, and gently swipe my lips over hers.

Charlie shoves at my shoulders, but I don't move until Rick Roman lifts me to my feet with a tap upside the back of my head. "Get off your girl so we can get these idiots into the van."

Looking around, I see the rest of the guys handcuffing the group of bumbling idiots who thought they had a chance to make big money from stealing people's identities.

The coincidence that this group of criminals found Charlie to target as Mac and Callan were plotting a scheme of their own is unbelievable, but here we are with me reaching a hand out to help her off the ground I plowed her down onto.

"Shit!!" I curse. "You okay, baby?"

She growls at me, then shoots me a pissed off look.

"I don't know if I hate you or love you right now."

"Can I pick then?"

"No!" she yells. "No, you cannot. I want to go home, and I want an explanation on the way."

Charlie has on her Miss Tyler mask, all bravado and strength, when I know she's about to go into shock and collapse.

"I'll take her," I say.

"No. I'm not going anywhere with you," she demands as she sinks down to the floor.

I reach for her and have her cuddled in my lap before her body even has time to hit the floor again. "Charlie, baby, you're going into shock," I say as her body shakes in my arms. "Let me take care of you and we can talk."

She shakes her head and Callan takes her from my grasp.

I plead with him with my tear-filled eyes, but I know this is for the best. It's the only reason I relinquish her into his care. "Black." My voice says it all, and he nods.

"Like she was Jordan."

I nod and throw my hands into my hair as my team collects the assholes around the room. Callan leaves the hotel room with Charlie's face in his chest, her body trembling in his arms.

When I arrive back at the condo complex, my heart aches as I open the door to my silent unit. I knew Charlie wouldn't be there, but I hoped until I turned the key in the lock and was met with an empty place.

Within minutes of arriving, a knocking on my door has me groaning because a lecture from Mac, Rick, and Dave is low on my list right now, but if experience means anything, that's what I'm about to get.

Sure enough, without fail, the three amigos enter without invitation and make themselves comfy in my living room.

"I didn't agree with Mac when he told us he was going along with Black's hairbrained scheme," Dave says. "I love the boy, but we all know he's not the best at making decisions in social situations."

Rick laughs. "I was with Dave until I saw your face. You love her." It's a statement, not a question.

I nod. "Yeah. Got blindsided, but yeah, I do."

Mac leaves the room and returns with a beer in his hand.

Handing it over to me, he sits next to me and places a hand on my leg. "I'm the first to be against anyone getting involved on the job." His eyes meet with Rick's. Mac dated Rick's sister when he was young and just starting out in the military. She was on their team and their relationship caused him to let his guard down. He paid the ultimate price, and Holly lost her life. Until he met his wife, Mac had thrown in the towel in the game of love, like me. "But you needed a change. The age bracket of pussy you were plowing through was starting to make you just look sad."

Mac smirks at me when I slowly turn my head to glower at him.

"What?" he asks. "I have daughters. I was just looking out for them."

"They're not even teenagers," I scoff.

"Can't ever be too safe."

I fling my head back on the sofa and sigh deeply. "What am I going to do? She's pissed that I lied to her. I'm not even sure how she knows, but she does, and I can't blame her. If I had explained and told her how I feel—"

"Would have, could have, should have," Rick interjects. "We've all been there. This job takes a toll and sometimes the decisions we're forced to make create problems in our personal lives. Do you think this girl can forgive you and handle shit in the future? If not, I hate to say it, but then you have a choice to make."

"I don't think you'll like the way I go with that."

The group collectively nods.

It's not long before Callan, Ace, and Elliot arrive, filling my small living room with their enormous bodies.

"Then let's figure out a way to make her understand," Dave offers.

Over the next couple hours, we plot and scheme like only trained operatives can and, by the time another knock pounds on my door, I think it can actually work.

Opening the door proves to be a poor choice because now I have seven screaming females, one of them only a teen, in my face—Anita, Emily, Jessie, Kayley, Montana, Sally, and Shana—demanding answers.

I lift my hands in front of my body for self-preservation. "Whoa!" I exclaim as the group of women swarms around me.

Anita is the first to speak, while Harold offers me a set of understanding eyes. "Listen here, Mr. Roland...we want the truth, and we want it now."

"Anita, sweetheart," her husband attempts to calm her. "I'm sure Storm has a very good reason for not being truthful."

I look at Callan, Ace, and Elliot and know my truth can't be the total story. Or so I'm thinking when Callan jumps in to save me.

"Elliot, Ace, and I are undercover operatives. We worked for the military for years, then went rogue. Storm worked on our team a time or two. I liked the dude. That doesn't happen very often. What happens even less is he treated me like a human being without being an asshole. Charlie did the same when we were kids." The room looks around at each other in confusion, but Callan is on a roll. "It made me think they'd be good together. I knew neither was happy with their love lives."

Emily takes Callan's hand and offers it a gentle squeeze. "You thought about how other people were feeling."

Callan nods with a slight smile on his lips. "I guess Jordan is rubbing off on me."

Emily, who mentions working with Callan's wife, Jordan, lets her boyfriend, Luke, tug her back from the fold surrounding me.

Sally, the next to speak, does so with a finger jabbing into my chest. "You made her happy and now she's broken and insisting she was foolish to let you in the way she did."

"She wasn't," I say. "She wasn't foolish and I don't want to see her broken. I'm going to do anything and everything to fix all of this. I never meant to hurt her. I didn't want to lie to any of you. I don't always have a choice with my...um, job."

Rourke pats my back on one side while Ian stands on the other. "She really likes you," Rourke begins. "But you know she struggles with control issues. She's just feeling out of control right now. She'll calm down and hear you out."

"I'd have a good explanation at the ready, though," Ian offers.

"Yeah," Brad adds. "Rourke usually spends hours writing his arguments down before he presents them to her. It involves alcohol, too. Lots of it."

"I can give you the Charlie bottle."

"That's what he calls it."

I smirk at the couple then the rest of the room. "I love her and I should have told her that from the start. I was ready to do it at the festival. I had this grand gesture playing out in my head all day. Had I just spoken the words, all of this could have been avoided."

"It's not your fault her identity was stolen and the psychos who took it also took her," Sally says.

"No, but my connection to her and my job made that happen."

"We always knew you boys were badass mother—"

"Alright, Neet," Harold says. "That's enough spiked cider for you. Let's go home and you and your sister can yip on the line about this until the cows come home."

"Anita, Harold," Mac says. "Can we have a moment of your time?"

The older couple nods and follows Mac and Dave into my kitchen. Rick left with the Lime Peak cops to file the report on the gang of idiots whose plan to steal money from Charlie didn't end the way they wanted.

It isn't long before Charlie's gaggle of friends arrive.

Shana and Kayley offer me kind smiles seconds before Jessie flings herself into my arms, her tears instantly wetting my shirt.

"Jess," Montana, her sister soothes with gentle circles on her back. "You just saw Miss T, remember? She's fine."

Into my chest, the young girl sobs words I can't make out, but I know she needs reassuring that everything is going to be okay.

"Shh," I whisper. "You're alright, Jessie. Baby, look at me, you're safe. You didn't do anything wrong. Those were bad men that wanted Miss T's money and took it without asking. When they thought they could get more, they came here looking for her, but me and my friends," I nod toward Callan, Ace, and Elliot, who each in kind lift a hand to Jessie in a wave, "caught them and now they're in jail. They're not coming back, and they'll never hurt you or Miss T again, I promise."

Jessie heaves in a gulp of air, but then finally settles.

I hand her back over to her sister and plop down again on my sofa, lowering my head into my hands. "If you're all here, is Charlie alone? Is she okay?"

"We told her we'd stay in shifts over the next few days. She fell asleep, so we all popped over. I'm on my way back now," Kayley says with a sad expression.

"I need to make this right," I state. "I need her back."

"And that's why we're here," Ian says.

Sally laughs. "It's cute you think that Ian, but no. That's why *we're* here." Sally points to herself and the other females in the room.

Charlie

Rourke tries to talk me into taking a few days off, but I refuse and show up at the admin building at my customary time before everyone else to find Ace perched on the hood of his car.

With hands in front of his body, he heads in my direction. "Don't be mad, but Storm wants you safe. I'm on perimeter duty. Monte is inside walking the halls, and Callan is going to be in your office with you today. Storm promises to give you space, but he can't relinquish control of your safety altogether."

I roll my eyes, but the gesture does something to my heart. It shows he understands actions speak louder than words and I'm his top priority even when I'm not speaking to him.

Storm hurt me. I knew the minute I found out he lied, he'd be sorry for what he did and try to mend our relationship. Fixing things between us will become his highest priority after my safety.

"Okay," I whisper. "Thanks."

Ace reaches for his phone and types a message before I turn to walk inside. My guess is that message is to Storm to let him know I've arrived and didn't fight having the guys here today.

I'm happy about it.

I don't want to be alone right now. So much so, I allowed my friends to sit sentry in my apartment. I also forwent my morning run. Well, that had as much to do with Storm as it did not wanting to be on the trail alone because any of my friends would have gladly joined me.

Storm and I met on that trail and spent lots of time walking there after that. In my mind, it's sort of has become our place.

There is also a part of me that wonders if he'd be on the trail waiting for me. I couldn't decide if that was a motivator to get me there or a deterrent to avoid it.

I went with avoidance.

I'm not ready to see him just yet even though I'm dying to put eyes on him.

I'm slow to open the door to my office and walk into the space where all went wrong only a few days ago.

The danger is gone. The men who stole my identity then tried to force ransom money from the company Storm works for are in the custody of federal agents and not going to cause me anymore trouble. This doesn't mean I'm not feeling scared as I enter the place where they were when Jessie and I came in to use my bathroom.

But when I open the door, my breath hitches because the space looks nothing like it did on Saturday.

Everything is different.

The walls are painted a soft blue, the floor is a light hardwood, and my desk has a fish tank built into the front.

The gesture of the tank alone almost brings me to my knees.

"He was unstoppable," Callan states from his spot in the corner of my office in a new puffy chair that looks book reading ready. "This tank cost him a fortune. I hope the gesture isn't lost on you."

I nod. "I bet. He knows my dad and I shared a love for them. I have my dad's in my bedroom."

It's Callan's turn to nod. "Yeah, Roland mentioned that. He said it would be soothing, but he was hellbent on giving you different fish in this one."

"He's always trying to show me I have an identity all mine aside from my father's legacy."

"I know I'm not the best with social shit," Callan begins. "But he's genuinely sorry. He's excepting blame for not telling you who he was, but it's really not his fault. I should be the one owning up to this, not Storm."

"You had good intentions. It was just—"

"Yeah, my moral compass doesn't always point in the right direction, but I did what I did to help you both."

"I know, Cal, and I love you for it."

I take the big man into my arms and squeeze him until he softens into my embrace.

"You've always been a good friend to me," Callan says. "Even when I didn't care about having any. Storm was always nice to me, too. I just thought it was a sign you two were meant for each other. He still thinks you guys are."

When I don't say anything, Callan continues.

"Anyway, I'm here to make sure you feel safe, nothing else. Roland actually made me promise not to bother you about your relationship, so I'm just going to sit over there in my corner and be quiet."

That has me laughing out loud. Callan Black has never been silent a day in his life.

He sends me a knowing smirk. "I already checked. You don't have a squirrel problem, so I should be all set with my lips sealed."

"Ah, huh. Okay. I'll believe that when I see it."

From his bag, the neurodivergent man extracts coffee and enough sweets to take down a horse.

He promptly makes quick time of setting up his treats, then offers me a bag with a few goodies of my own.

I take the proffered goods and dive in greedily. Chewing, I say through a bite, "Colleen and Olivia have a knack for desserts and hot beverages, don't they?"

"Hits the spot every time."

"Mmm."

He isn't wrong.

After consuming what I can only guess is my weight in sugar and calories, the edginess of my nerves floats away. By the time Callan is asking me if I want to place an order with him for lunch—for a man in tiptop shape, you'd never guess the way he eats—I'm feeling almost like myself again.

When Montana and Jessie arrive at half-past two asking me to take a walk with them, I jump at the chance to stretch my legs and fill my lungs with some much-needed fresh air.

"We can only do a quick walk," Jessie reports as she glances at her watch she was so proud to buy with her own money earned working in the camp's preschool. "It's going to get dark soon, then it won't be safe."

Montana leans into my side and whispers, "Go along with it. Ryan has a surprise planned."

I look at Jessie's sister with wide eyes, then smile when she winks.

"So, how are things going?" I ask the young teacher who donates her school vacation days to us at the camp.

"The Titans were projected to win the Super Bowl," she scoffs. "But we all know how that ended. The guys are way too cocky for my comfort. Felix Tibet, their tight end, is leading the ego train. The guy is such a douche."

I eye her suspiciously and Montana smirks. "I never said he wasn't stupid hot. All I'm saying is, his head is as big as he claims his dick is."

"Ohhh!" Jessie giggles. "You said the bad word for..." She lowers her voice to a whisper and blushes before saying, "Penis."

Montana and I giggle along with her as we make it to the entrance of the trail on the camp side. I usually enter on the opposite side, so at least this walking route will differ from what I did with Storm.

That doesn't mean he's not all I'm thinking about as our breaths catch when we see the fairy lights lining the ground down a side path.

"Jessie," I say, excitement for her lacing my voice. "Look at Ryan in his suit from the dance. He really planned a big surprise for you."

"I know, Miss T. Ryan told me."

Montana and I laugh. Of course, the boy told her his secret before she was surprised.

Jessie doesn't seem to mind, though. "He's asking me to be executive."

Montana chuckles, then corrects her sister. "Exclusive, Jess. He's asking you to be exclusive."

"Yeah, that's what I said. We're not just Netflixing and chilling."

That has my chuckles adding to the merriment until Ryan takes my hand in one of his with Jessie's in the other and says, "You come with me."

"Me?" I ask. "Ryan, why don't you and Jessie go on ahead alone? You'll be okay for a few minutes as long as you don't go too far into the path."

"No!" Jessie exclaims with much too much oompah for me not to wonder what the problem is.

"Jessie." Montana says her sister's name in a scolding voice. "Remember we talked about the plan."

"Oh, yeah. Okay. Miss T, you need to come with us because his hormones are running wild for all of this." She does a little dance as she slides her hands down her sides. "Now that we're execution."

"We need to work on that word," I say, then shrug and let the excited teens lead me into the path.

We're not ten steps in when a lump forms in my throat and my heart drops to my feet as I see the real reason Ryan and Jessie wanted me to come into the woods with them to see the lights.

The fairy lights on either side of the ground open, and it's like a magical wonderland before me as the sun sets and the lights blink in the growing darkness. They hang from a tree a few feet in front of me with glowing hearts where leaves will be in a few months.

All of it is enough to take my breath away. But then I turn around and see Jessie and Ryan, hand in hand, leaving the woods in the direction we entered. When I turn back to the sparking lights, I almost fall to my knees.

Storm Roland strolls out—hands deep in his pockets, beanie on his head—from behind the massive tree and leans against it.

His knee bends and his foot rests on the trunk. "Charlene." He says my full name.

He pushes off the tree to come stand inches from me.

It's only been two days since I touched him, but it feels like an eternity when his bare hand, cold but soothing, touches my cheek.

"I'm glad you came. I'd like the chance to talk and explain. Tell you what I should have days ago. Will you stay and hear me out?"

I nod as tears threaten to fall.

Storm takes my hand and leads me a little to the right, off the path to where he's set up camp.

There's a table with electric candles for safety, a tent with twinkling lights glowing from inside, and a hammock with more pillows and blankets than a Pottery Barn catalog display.

"I'd like to hold you in my arms while I explain." Storm nods in the hammock's direction.

"Scared I'll bolt?"

He lets out a low grumble from his chest. "Yeah. Honestly, I am."

I allow him to take my hand and lead me to the hammock.

Storm climbs on. He's agile and makes it look so easy.

When it's my turn, I'm relieved when he leans over and scoops me up.

"Umph." I groan when I land atop his hard body, my front to his.

"Sorry," he says. "Don't always know my strength. That's probably why Jessie told her sister I look like The Hulk."

"What?" I ask with a giggle.

A handsome smile spreads across Storm's face. "She's a good girl. Ryan's a great kid, too. They helped me with this, you know?"

"I suspected once I saw you."

"Montana's a piece of work, huh?"

I chuckle. "You picked up on that already?"

"From the first introduction."

Storm readjusts us with a deep male groan and an apology for the erection that's now deliciously pressing into my back.

Now, don't get me wrong. I'm still hurt. I'm still angry. And I'm still scared of a relationship with Storm after he spent weeks hiding information and his true identity from me.

But I'm also pretty sure I'm in love with the man and right now, nothing feels better than his muscular arms around me, his soft breath in my ears, and his hard dick pressing into the crease of my ass.

"Does Daddy need to remind you of your manners?" he asks, his voice more cautious than usual. "You be nice and quiet and hear me out, then you can have your turn to say whatever you want."

"Is this really the time?" I ask.

I feel his shrug from behind. "Let's get one thing out of the way. You're not looking to have sex with your father, nor do you have Daddy issues. This is about the position of authority a father figure offers. Nothing more than the classic control and domination. But if you don't want to play while I explain—"

"No, Daddy, I want to play. I've missed our games."

Storm presses his erection into me and grinds it back and forth. "Me, too, little girl. Me, too."

Storm tilts my chin so our eyes meet, then he lowers and plants a gentle kiss to the tip of my nose.

"I'm accepting full responsibility for my actions and blame for what happened to you. I let my emotions impede my job and that put you in danger. That mistake was a one-off and will never happen again. When I watched the playback from the security cameras and heard you give yourself to them..." Storm's body shakes in anger and he growls. "What the fuck were you thinking? And regardless of the answer, after this thing between us is settled, you're getting your ass tanned for that."

"I couldn't let them touch Jessie. She understands some basics on sex, but—"

"Yeah, I heard what they called her and the gang rape promise. But, baby, you said you weren't going to fight them. Did they tou—"

"No! I was so scared." I sob uncontrollably as I turn in Storm's arms and plant my face in his chest. "I knew I had to do something to get her out of their heads, so I offered myself."

"You're going to make a great mom someday."

I look up into his eyes and see my future. Or at least I hope it's mine.

I nod. "It just came out without thinking. Once I said it, and they dragged me away, I didn't know what to do. They must have drugged me because I woke up in the hotel room with my clothes all still perfectly in place and not a sore spot on me."

The breath he releases is so deep and strong, he must have been holding it since he heard the alarm blare through campus. "Thank fuck, baby. You're Daddy's brave girl, though, aren't you?"

"Yes, Daddy," I say. "Maybe instead of that spanking I have coming, you should give me a reward."

Storm lets out a hearty laugh. It's a sound I've missed the last couple of days and it makes my heart nearly burst inside my chest.

"Let me explain first, then we'll see what else we need to take care of."

His hand slips down my belly and cups the heat of my pussy.

I moan and rock my hips before he pulls away.

"Callan organized our meeting because he means well, but he's out of his fucking mind, and, as you know, the social shit still isn't his area of expertise."

I laugh at that. "No, it's not. He attended Camp SubLime when we were kids and my dad was still alive. They formed a bond and kept in touch. He and I spoke occasionally, but Anita and him remained close even after my dad passed."

"She told him you were lonely and looking for something in a man you couldn't find. You know how he overthinks shit to the point of obsession? Well, he studied you and figured out you were meant to be a submissive in the bedroom, but dominant in your career. I haven't met her, but I understand his wife is the same."

"Jordan?" I ask. "Maybe. She's a psychologist. She's definitely able to handle Cal, so she's a strong woman."

"Black concocted the idea of hooking us up. Not sure how to make it happen, he ran a background check on you and found you had your identity stolen and someone was using your name, social, and the rest of your info to pretend they were you. When he figured out a way to kill two birds with one stone, he convinced our boss to play along and assign me to your case. He got protection for you while he, Mac, and the others found the guys and he threw us together and sat back and laughed when we did the rest of the work for him."

"It didn't feel like work to me," I say in a soft voice.

Storm hugs me tighter around my middle. "Not for me, either. This thing between us has been the easiest thing

I've ever done. It felt right to me since the second I opened your file."

I turn in his arms and send him a quizzical look. "And what did this file include?"

He chuckles. "Pictures that had me jerking off so hard, when I came, I knew I was in trouble. And I knew I had to have you." Storm brings his lips to mine. "I'm sorry I didn't tell you who I was and why I came to Lime Peak. Once we started our thing, I should have been honest with you. I want you to know, I never suspected you were involved in smuggling drugs."

I laugh. "I hope not. It's laughable, Storm. If you believed that, I'd have to question your investigative skills."

Storm tugs me under him and the hammock sways. "Are you questioning Daddy, little girl?"

His lips meet mine again. This time, I open for him, and he groans into our embrace.

Our kiss turns into heaving petting as his hand clasps a breast and his hips push his erection into my core.

He rocks his hips and slides back and forth over my slit. "So, the Daddy thing?"

Storm smiles. "Yes? What do you want to know?"

"Have you always been into it?"

He emits a sigh. "My brother married his college sweetheart. Mine didn't work out, and I started fucking my way through life. As I got older, the girls got younger. Recently, it was starting to be pointed out to me it was getting sad. But the kink we play with? Nah, that's new. I mean, the basic concept of Daddy kink works for us, right? I'm more sexually experienced compared to you. I'm the one in charge, putting the rules in place and making sure you obey. With you, my daddy fetish also includes protection and soothing elements, such as encouraging you to behave a certain way, like being brave and confident in yourself. And I'll always reward you for doing what you're told."

"Look!" I exclaim as moisture hits my face. "It's snowing."

Storm looks over his shoulder up to the sky. "Beautiful, but nothing compares to you. Please tell me I didn't fuck this up?"

"You didn't fuck this up...too badly."

Storm laughs. "So, I can make it up to you inside that tent over there?"

I nod. "Yes. It's too cold to stay out and watch the snow, even though it's romantic and would be perfect to make love under."

Storm rolls off the hammock, then tugs me into his arms and marches for the tent.

Placing me on my feet in the glowing warmth, he points to the ceiling. It's clear so we can watch the snow fall from the safety of a covering.

I'm mesmerized by the beauty of it, but then I turn and my breath hitches.

Storm is bent on one knee with a small square velvet box in his palm.

I lift my hand to my mouth to catch the cry I know is on its way. When Storm takes my hand and speaks, it's useless and my tears flow freely down my face.

"Charlie," he says. "I know this is insanely fast and, frankly, insane, but I love you. I want you and no one but you. What I did was wrong, and I'm so sorry for hurting you. You can trust me and know I will never lie or omit anything for as long as I live. I want to be your husband. I want to love you and take care of you. I want you in my arms all night, every night and I want to be inside you every second you'll let me. Be my wife. Do this craziness with me, Charlie, please."

I wrap his face in my hands and lower to my knees in front of him. "Storm," I cry. "Oh, my god. Are you serious?"

He takes my face into his hands, too, and brings our lips together. "Yes. Totally serious. Marry me," he says with our lips touching.

Opening, his tongue licks over mine and I moan into his mouth. Pulling back, I break our kiss to say, "Yes. Yes, I'll do this craziness with you."

He slips the ring on my hand and the feel of it surrounding my finger brings a sense of security to me. I know with him I will always be safe and cared for, loved and cherished.

Storm's eyes heat with love like I've never known, but behind that love there's something dark and devious brewing and I smirk, knowing one request is all it will take to kick him into the role I'm looking for.

"Daddy," I say with the tip of my index finger in my mouth. "I was naughty, wasn't I? With those bad men that scared me."

"Jesus fuck, Charlie." He grunts. "Yeah? I'm game if you are and if this is what you need."

I nod. It is. I need to let it go and I can't think of a better or more fun way than letting Storm punish me.

"I'm not going to go at you easy, little girl."

"Give me your best shot." I purr at the thought of him coming at me hard.

"On the bed," he orders. "And don't move."

I smirk Storm's way, then do as he asks, sitting on the bed and waiting for my next instruction.

"Oh," he says. "I see how this is going to go. You're going to be a brat. You know I meant lie down, but seeing as how you're being fresh, why don't we start with something else? Stand," he orders as he sits in the camping chair and crooks a finger at me. "Strip for me."

I know he means for me to take off my clothes and then get on the bed the way he demanded, but I'm feeling bratty, so I push my hand down firmly into his chest to let him know I'm in charge...if only for a few minutes.

I lean down and give him a quick kiss, a sweep of my lips over his.

Storm moans and grabs the nape of my neck like a mother cat would do to her kitten. I purr like one and it doesn't go unnoticed.

"You want to be my kitten, baby?"

"Yes, Daddy."

Storm's hand pets the hair on the top of my head then drags it down the side, tucking a strand behind my ear.

Slowly, I pull away to seductively walk a few steps from him, wiggling my ass as I do. Then I stop, look over my shoulder and slowly reach for the zipper of my coat. Lowering it before letting it fall off my shoulders, I shiver.

"If you're cold, I'll raise the heat."

Of course he outfitted the tent with an electric heater so I'd be comfortable.

"No." He lifts an eyebrow and I add what he's looking for. "Daddy. I'm okay, just...you, you know?"

"I do, Kitten. You make me shiver, too. Look at this," he says as he unzips his fly and extricates his tip. "This is what you do to me."

Using this new nickname does something to the pulsing of my blood and I can't break my gaze as his fist grips his strong erection through his pants and strokes himself. When Storm moans, I bring my eyes to him, and we lock stares.

Holding it, I take a step back toward him and put my hands on my hips. "I want you to get naked with me. It'll be way more fun that way."

Storm smiles. "I'll play along. You first. Show me yours, baby, and I'll show you mine."

First comes my shoes. I toe them off before tugging each sock loose.

Storm does the same as his eyes remain glued to mine.

And slowly, I lower my pants to the floor. As I do, I bend to give him the best view of my ass.

He slowly opens the zipper of his jeans, drawing my eyes to the large bulge fighting to escape.

Storm's eyes meet mine with a knowing wink. "Like what you see?"

"Yes, Daddy."

"It's all yours," he says, wiggling his hips to free his jeans from his body.

Cupping his package and giving it a little tug, I moan at the lewd sight.

"Let me see," I beg.

With a smile, Storm removes his boxer briefs and frees his enormous cock.

It's the most perfect dick, long and thick with a bulbous head that turns almost purple just above the ridge he loves me to circle my tongue over when he's aroused.

As my hands return to my hips, I slowly rotate them in a circle as I let my head swing in the opposite direction.

Storm grunts through a few rough strokes of his hand over his cock. The head is deep purple and a bead of pre-cum drips from the tip until he swipes over it with the pad of his thumb.

When I get close enough to touch, he tries to grab me, but I playfully swat his hands away. "Hands down, no touching," I warn.

"Oh, you make the rules now, little girl, huh?"

I smile and shyly nod.

"Okay. I'll play along because I am sorry for not telling you the truth when we met, but I hope this is going to be worth it for you. The more you tease me, the more you'll be teased."

Shrugging, I straddle his leg, seductively grinding my pussy on him

"Mmm." He hums. "That pussy is so hot and wet. I want my mouth on it, baby. I want to taste you."

I shake my head and slowly walk backward, away from him, stopping a few feet away. Slowly, I turn my back to him. Slipping the shoulder straps of my bra down before undoing it, I dangle it off a finger before dropping it to the floor.

"Get rid of the fucking panties and bring that wet pussy back over here. I want you to get yourself off and come on my leg."

Obediently, I sit down on his knee and start grinding again, finding my rhythm immediately and charging headfirst into a climax I've been desperate to have for days.

"Daddy?" I call out as I circle my hard clit with my fingers while I rub back and forth on Storm's leg.

"Your daddy's right here," he says as his mouth finds my earlobe. "Can you feel me, Char?"

"Yes."

"Where?"

"Everywhere," I admit. "Oh, god! Storm, I'm so close."

"I know, baby."

I moan as I rub myself over his leg, my hands finding his shoulders for purchase as my orgasm moves into sight.

Flinging my head back, I scream his name as I start to unravel.

"Fucking hell! Watching you get yourself off is incredibly hot, Kitten. That's my good girl. Come for me. Come for Daddy."

I do.

I come for him...hard and fast. I come, uninhibited and comfortable in my skin. I come for what feels like hours but only seconds, then without thinking, I sink to my knees and nudge open Storm's legs to fit between them. Fisting his cock, I shove his hand away and take over, never missing a beat.

"I'm about ready to come, baby. Go 'head and finish me off, then we'll start over. Give me your mouth, Kitten. Make me purr."

Opening my mouth. I lower it over his crown and take him in deep.

His hands enter my hair, one on the side of my face, the other on the top of my head, to hold me on his cock as he thrusts up into my mouth.

I relax my throat and allow him to glide in and out over my tongue, giving him a nip of teeth on the way back in.

"Such a good mouth," Storm praises. "Such a good fucking mouth. Going to make Daddy come in it. And I want you to wait until you're told to swallow. I want to feel me go down your throat. I want to feel you swallow my load," Storm says, as he wraps his palms around my neck. "Keep sucking like that."

There is something about his powerful hands as he grips me tightly with passion that makes me feel secure and desired. It's pure bliss as I float into a euphoric state.

I keep my pace steady, sucking him into the deep recesses of my throat while my tongue flicks at his underside.

Storm grunts and curses in half sentences through it all until he stills and retreats a little. "Here it comes. Fucking hell, I'm going to come so hard."

Storm fills my mouth with his warm release, and I hold it there until he finishes unloading himself.

"Swallow," he orders as he squeezes my throat to feel me gulp him down. One swallow isn't enough, and he chuckles when he feels me work the rest of him down before I lick my lips. "God damn, woman."

"Good, Daddy?"

Storm pulls me into his body with his hands returning to my head. This time, it's to cuddle me close and plant a soft kiss to my temple, then to my forehead. "The best. I love you. Now, let me make love to you."

With a single nod, Storm takes me to my feet, then into his arms.

He walks us to the bed and gently places me down, his body following mine the entire way. His weight is like a blanket, providing the pressure I need to be grounded and set myself free.

I watch as the soft, white snow falls gently from the sky and sigh into his neck, my tongue licking the strong column.

He returns the action with a nibble of my ear before he brings our gazes together. "Watch as I slide into you. Home where I belong. Inside you, where I was always meant to be. You were made for me, Charlene Tyler, and now you're all mine."

"I've been yours since the day you plowed me over on the trail."

Storm laughs. "Not my finest moment. But I promise this is."

Resting his forearms on the mattress to trap my head between, our eyes remain locked, and he pushes forward, gaining entry with a moan. "Fucking perfect pussy, you have. Feels so fucking tight around me, baby. So fucking tight."

I arch when I feel the invasion, the pinch of the stretch as he slowly pulls out. "You're so thick, it fills me, stretches so good."

Storm grunts through his next thrusts. "How I'm hard after coming like that, I can't explain, but fuck me, Charlie, this is what you do to me."

Storm settles us into a rhythm designed for the long haul. After the orgasm he's had, I know his next isn't soon to hit and I welcome the soreness I'm sure to have in the morning.

He shifts to get deeper, placing my leg over his hip, then bringing it to his shoulder. "Yes," I cry out when the tip of his dick nudges into a spot deep inside me that feels so good. "Right there."

Storm's mouth lowers to capture my cries of pleasure as he stays working that glorious spot until my toes curl and heat shoots from my feet to my head.

With my skin flush and hot, another climax begins in my core. "Storm, I'm going to come."

"That's my good girl. Give it to me. I love the way it feels when you come on my cock. So fucking wet and tight. Makes holding back so fucking hard."

His hand slides between us, and he flicks at my hardened clit with his tongue and I come so hard, I miss a second in time.

Coming to, my body still thumping to our in sync heart beats, I wrap both legs around his waist and grind up into him.

Storm growls. "So good. Don't want to come yet, though. I want to be inside you forever."

"We have forever," I say. "Come inside me, now. I want to feel you."

"Jesus, Kitten. I love you."

"Love you."

A few shifts and thrusts later, Storm roars through his climax.

It floods me. Fills me deep with a warmth—only Storm gives me—through my blood and bones, to my heart and soul.

Our lips meet and we kiss like lovers who want to get so close we're under the other's skin.

Our kissing turns into more sex and that sex turns into dirty sex then sweet and passionate lovemaking until the animals in the forest wake and the stars fade away for the rise of the sun.

Storm

Our night in the woods was amazing, but this morning topped the cake with some of the best sex of my life.

My ring on Charlie's finger was just as much a turn on as the taste of me between her legs when I went down on her to wake her with an orgasm.

Flinging her body over mine as she woke, so her pussy covered my face, I guided her head to my dick and thrusted up into her waiting mouth.

Once we were both ready, I positioned her on her knees and gave her the spanking punishment she had coming. By the time I slid my cock into her from behind as she was coming from nothing more than my hand slapping her ass, she was good and red and wouldn't be able to sit anytime soon without remembering the spanking she took like a seasoned champ.

Now, after a quick stop at the condo for a shower—together, which led to more great sex—we climb into my truck for a road trip to my brother's.

We stop at Anita's sister's place in Falls Village for a hearty breakfast to tide us over for the long ride to Edgemont, where my twin, Corey, lives with his family.

Edgemont is an ethnically diverse inner suburb of New York City, populated with strip malls, gas stations, and outlet stores. It was originally a development designed by different architects for summer homes for Manhattanites with antique colonial homes and outstanding schools, which is why my brother and Delaney picked it as their home with my niece and nephew.

Corey can get into the city in less than half an hour for work, if needed, but his kids are growing up in a safe suburb with some of the best schools.

"So you live in the next town over?" Charlie asks.

"Yeah, both Corey and I have office space in White Plains. I live there."

"And you promise Corey and Delaney aren't going to think you're crazy for moving to Maine for a girl you just met?"

We talked through our living arrangements last night and decided on Maine because Charlie needs to stay there for her job at Camp Sublime. I can work remote from anywhere while my office managers run my offices. I already have two running successfully without me on site most of the time.

I laugh, a hearty one from the pit of my belly. "Oh, they think I'm nuts, but once you meet my other brother, you'll see why this thing between us is no big deal."

"Other brother?" she asks as we make our way through Connecticut, getting ready to stop for gas and to maybe grab a quick sandwich for lunch.

"Yeah. Corey and I are twins, but my parents had a surprise baby. Rhodes attends Tulane in Louisiana."

"Oh, wow! He's a lot younger than you."

"Hey," I scold with a smile. "I'm not that old."

"You're old enough to be his father."

"Let's not forget I'm your Daddy and I can pull this truck over and remind you what that means."

I smirk as she shifts uncomfortably in her seat. I lit up her ass good this morning, so I turn up the seat heaters on her side of the vehicle.

"Are you and Corey identical?"

"Yes, but we don't look all that much alike anymore. He's in great shape but lean to my beefiness."

Charlie reaches across the seat and squeezes my biceps as I flex. "You're crazy."

"Crazy for you," I quip, then lean into her space and kiss her on the lips. "But like the typical frat boy, Rhodes is his own level of crazy. He has it bad for his best friend's little sister, who happens to be a freshman at Tulane."

A knowing eyebrow raise from Charlie has me chuckling. "How's that going?"

I shrug. "Last I heard, they're friends with benefits behind Forest's back, so it should go bad any second, if it hasn't already. I'm not totally up to date on everything because my family thought I was deployed and couldn't take calls. They don't know about the undercover gig. They think I'm still in the service."

Charlie turns her entire body to face me, and I know what I'm about to hear. "Storm!" She admonishes.

"I know, I know. I'm going to tell them as much as I can. It's not like I'm lying for me. There's stuff in this line of work that I can't share with them. Stuff I won't be able to share with you. We've been over this. It's for your own safety if I keep something from you." It was another conversation we had last night.

Charlie emits a low growl as I pull off in a coastal town on the train line known for it's busy Main Street in the center of town.

"Let's get gas and grab a soup and sandwich. I know this great place right around here."

I maneuver us through the gas station where I grab a few snacks for the ride home tomorrow and then deal with the traffic down Post Road to the famous soup spot.

Parking, I get out and open Charlie's door. Taking her hand, we walk inside and place our soup order—mulligatawny for me, classic chicken noodle for her—to go because we're going to grab a sandwich down the road then head to a nearby park to eat outside in the crisp winter air.

At the deli that's been feeding people since 1970, I get a red dragon panini with grilled chicken, cheddar, avocado, banana peppers, and red chili mayo on a hard roll while Charlie orders a grilled cheese from the kids' menu and teases me about our kink.

I pull my sassy girl to my side and lean down to whisper into her ear. "Be Daddy's good girl. I don't think this luscious ass," I say as I let my hand slip over her globes, then pat her slightly, "can handle anymore."

Charlie's breath hitches as I take her hand in my free one, our sandwiches in the other, and lead her back to my car.

It's a quick ride to the park that sits by a small pond where a few picnic tables wait for people to stop by and enjoy their day.

I brush the light dusting of soft snow from the bench and sit Charlie next to my side so she'll be warm.

She gets to opening our food quickly while I throw a blanket I always keep in my truck around our shoulders.

"This is nice. It's chilly, but nice," Charlie says. Then, "So, you mentioned once that your brother and his wife split up for a while. What's the story there so I don't put my foot in my mouth?"

I'm glad she asked because Corey and Lainey's story is one that definitely lends to feet being put into one's mouth.

I smirk when I think back through the few years with my brother and sister-in-law and how they reunited after sneaking around and getting caught by their teenage children having kitchen sex.

"Mmm." I hum when the hot soup filled with spices, vegetables, apple, lentils, tomato paste, and rice hits my taste buds.

"Good?" Charlie asks. "I've always wondered what mulligatawny was. I'm not all that adventurous with my food."

"Here." I offer her a spoonful. "It's a sweet and spicy soup with a heavy Indian influence. Some make it soupier like this one, other places make theirs more rustic and chunkier like a stew with chunks of chicken."

Charlie takes a cautious sip. "You're making me into a whole new woman."

"I don't want to ever change you, Charlie. I love you just the way you are."

I'm awarded with the best smile that lights up my day and will be there for me every day until I take my last breath.

"Want more?" I ask. "It'll keep you warm out here."

"Nah." She brushes my offer off. "One taste was enough for me. Too spicy. I'll stick to my chicken noddle. Do you want some of mine?"

I shake my head and take a bite of my sandwich.

"So, Corey and Delaney?" she prompts.

I sigh. "They met when we were in college. Love at first sight kind of thing. They made it strong for a long time, then Lainey's dad died suddenly, and it messed with her head."

I see the moisture in Charlie's eyes. "Hmm."

Taking her hand in mine, I give it a gentle squeeze. "It sucks. I know it's not easy for you either, baby. Please promise me you'll always let me know what you need from me. That's where Lainey went wrong and then my brother was an epic idiot. While they were separated, he started dating this horrible young chick who worked for him. We all called her Poison Ivy."

"That's terrible." Charlie giggles. "Was her name Ivy, at least."

"Yeah, and she was horrible."

We finish eating and I make quick time of cleaning up because it is cold as hell out here.

Returning to my truck for the rest of the ride, Charlie fiddles with the radio as I climb into my seat.

"But they're back together?" she asks.

I chuckle. "Yeah."

Charlie smiles as we cross into New York and head to my apartment.

I've only been in the place for one night, so I can't imagine what she's going to think when she sees the mess I left.

Corey rented the place when he and Delaney separated. He lived there for a couple years, all the while putting in minimal effort into making it livable. The poor guy never wanted to be there in the first place. Corey spent their time apart acting like a fool with a ridiculous girl, all the while pining for his wife. He only made that minimal effort for his kids. Their rooms were comfortable, the rest of the place hardly felt lived in.

When I moved my shit in, I tossed boxes on the floor and pretty much called it a day. I thought I'd have time to unpack, but then the call came in from Mac and I headed to Lime Peak.

I explain all this as best as I can before I unlock the door to my place, but I don't think Charlie was prepared for the disarray we find.

"Wow! Are you sure no one broke in here?"

I laugh. "Nope. It's organized chaos. I know where everything—well, most things are. Come on, let me show you around. Watch your step," I warn.

I give Charlie the tour as I collect stuff in a bag I want for now. The rest I'll have shipped to me in Maine once Charlie and I have our living arrangements decided. At least it's already boxed up.

We haven't worked all of that out yet. I don't want to be presumptuous, but when we return to Maine in a few days, we'll be living together.

Neither of our condos is ideal for two people, so if I get my way, we'll be house hunting next week. Once that's situated, I'll send for my things.

Charlie looks around, picking up and putting down items. She hums over a few and asks some questions.

Then it's time to meet Corey and his family at The Tipsy Pig.

I hold the door open for Charlie and let her enter ahead of me. Once in the restaurant, I take her by the hand and lead her to the table where my twin and his family waits.

Liam, my teenage nephew, sits slumped in his chair with his arms crossed over his chest and a scowl on his face while Addie, his sister, talks animatedly to her mother.

"Hey," I say as we reach the table. "Gang, this is Charlene Tyler. She prefers Charlie. My fiancée."

Lainey stands and instantly takes Charlie into her arms. "I'm so glad you're here. I've been dealing with the three Roland boys on my own since college. I need a sidekick. Whatever it costs for you to overlook his bullshit, Corey can pay it. Now let me see the ring."

"Hey!" my brother and I scoff simultaneously.

"Peeps," Corey says, using his nickname for his wife. "I don't have that kind of money."

Lainey and my niece are squealing with Charlie over her diamond while I punch the asshole in the arm, then smirk when Corey winces and rubs the spot of contact. "You've got more money than you let on, and Charlie loves my bullshit, don't you, Spunky?"

Charlie rolls her eyes, then turns to Delaney. "What kind of money are we talking about?"

Lainey giggles as she sits back down. "I like her. Can we keep her?"

"No! She's mine."

Lainey sticks her tongue out at me then turns to Charlie. "I almost forgot to ask, how was the sauce?"

Charlie smirks, then turns and winks in my direction.

"Sauce?" my brother asks. "Peep's sauce? It's the best."

Knowing I can't avoid it, I sigh and admit, "I called Lainey—"

"In full-on panic mode," Lainey unhelpfully adds with a chuckle and a return wink for Charlie.

"Core—"

"No!" my brother yells at his wife, then softens his voice. "Sorry, it's not your fault. But I'm not having the disrespect for either of us. And he needs a minute to chill out."

Corey has Liam by the back of his shirt and out the door before my sister-in-law can respond.

"Family life isn't easy," Lainey admits. "I guess it's good you guys see this now. I know it's exciting doing a whirlwind romance, love at first sight kind of thing, but this is the reality. The infatuation dies, and if you don't have a love and respect for the other, surviving long-term won't happen."

I take Charlie's hand in mine. "You in for the long haul, Kitten?"

"Messy stuff and all."

I kiss her temple and we place an order for the table that arrives right around the time my brother returns with Liam looking sullen and like he's been crying.

My nephew apologizes to the table and hugs his mother before tucking into his meal.

After Corey and I argue over who's paying the bill—the women tell us to put our dicks away and split the tab—Charlie and I follow them to their house.

Liam runs to his room without a word and Addie does the same, but with a shy wave before hurling herself up the stairs.

My sister-in-law sighs in relief.

"If people ever tell you to have babies because they're cute and fun, please remember everything you witnessed tonight."

Charlie and I share a nervous laugh. I may have put a ring on it, but I'm not sure we're ready for that just yet. However, the thought of her pregnant with my child does something caveman like to me.

To change the subject and distract my mind from every way I could mark Charlie as mine, I ask, "So what went down with Liam and the girlfriend?"

Corey smirks and Lainey groans.

"What?" I ask my brother.

"Well, you know how it is at their age for guys. The poor kid is dating this smoking hot girl and trying to deal with his hormones. He's walking around..." Corey clears his throat then looks at Lainey and warns, "Cover your ears, Peeps. He's walking around with a hard-on all day and jerking off all night. I've had numerous talks with him, bought him condoms, even watched videos with the freaking kid."

"Wait," Delaney asks. "What?" Corey tries to wave her off, but my sister-in-law is like a dog without a bone and has to know everything. "You watched porn with our baby?"

Corey sighs. "First, he's not a baby anymore and hasn't been for a very long time. Second, no, I did not watch porn, I watched an informational video with him about the changes to his body, the things to know about a woman's body—which I have to say, if we had videos like this back in the day, we could have saved a lot of girls from the bumbling and fumbling we did..."

"Speak for yourself," I say. "I've always been a master at sex."

"Hold up." Lainey raises a hand. "You're teaching him how to be a master at sex? My little boy?"

"Again, Peeps, he's not little anymore. Actually, speaking of...Marley told her friends Liam is hung and doesn't..." His eyes go to his wife's in search of the right word. "Um, finish as fast anymore when her hand is in his pants."

Lainey lays her head on the kitchen table where we've gathered for conversation and a few beers.

I laugh. "Good for him."

"So his girlfriend told her friends, and they spread it around because they're jealous?" Charlie asks.

"I don't know. I never thought about it that way," Corey admits.

"No. He's too busy gloating over the fact his son has a big dick and can last when a girl gives him a hand job. Think long and hard about marrying into this family, Charlie. Long and hard."

"Long and hard being the family slogan."

My brother and I high-five.

"I mean, except for Rhodes," I add with a laugh.

Lainey and Charlie roll their eyes in unison.

"Leave him alone," Delaney warns.

Corey rolls his eyes now and then explains to Charlie that Rhodes was just a baby when he and Lainey started dating, so she's always had a soft spot for him.

"Storm said he's in college and likes his best friend's little sister?"

"Yeah, he's an ass. The DNA was used up by the time our parents had their little accident they like to refer to as a surprise."

"Well, if history repeats itself, he should fuck shit up with Lake any day now and come running to us for help."

Of course, Lainey steps in to defend him. "Or you'll meet him at his graduation in May. He's not sure what he's doing about a job or where to go after. This thing with Lake and Forest is really throwing him for a loop. She's younger and has three more years of school in Louisiana."

Charlie hums. "It's hard to blend lives to be sure everyone's needs are met."

Her eyes meet mine.

I clear my throat. "Speaking of...um, I have something to tell you," I start. "I retired from the military a long time ago, and I've been working for an undercover private security company of sorts ever since. A couple of the guys live up in Maine and with Charlie there—"

"Oh!" Lainey exclaims. "You're moving?"

"What about your business?" Corey asks, then socks me in the arm. "That's for fucking lying to us."

"I deserve that. I'm sorry. It's not something I'm supposed to be talking about to anyone. But I'm cutting back in the field and thinking about running my business remotely while my office managers handle the day-to-day. Hey, you guys can come up and take the kids skiing."

"We have golf courses there, too," Charlie adds. "Storm says you guys love to play."

Lainey scoffs. "That's an understatement."

My brother yanks her into his lap and nuzzles her neck. "Or we can ship the kids off to Uncle Storm and Auntie Charlie, and we can fuck right here."

Lainey tries to bat him away but ends up giggling instead. She kisses the tip of my brother's nose. "But I never regretted any decision I made that kept us together. If you guys truly love one another, you'll be happy anywhere you are as long as it's together."

Corey sinks his fingers into her hair and drags his lips over his wife's. When she opens for him, they groan until they come up for air.

Corey shifts in his seat, Lainey still on his lap, and looks at me. "Leave so I can fuck my wife now."

I laugh. "Go to your room at least," I order. "I don't need my niece and nephew calling me again to tell me they found the two of you doing it in here."

Corey stands and puts Lainey on her feet. "Call me in the morning. We can get a round in with the guys at Full Swing Ahead before you guys leave."

Lainey brings Charlie into a hug then walks us to the door. "We can do nails and get coffee with my mom after I drop the kids off for their activities. Come here with Storm and we'll head out after they leave."

After firming up plans and thanking our hosts, Charlie and I return to my apartment.

I want her in my bed, and we need to rest a few hours before spending the day with Corey and Lainey, but I also need to pack a few more things into the truck so after golf for us guys and nails for the girls, Charlie and I can head back to Maine. She needs to be on site at the camp for the work week and she has her routine the night before, I don't want to disrupt.

I search through my closet for the item I don't want to forget.

Finding the black bag, I pull it from its spot and lift my chin in Charlie's direction. "I have something I want to show you. Have a seat."

Obeying quickly, she sits on the corner of the bed, hands obediently in her lap. "What is it?"

"My Dom bag. I trained with a Dominant specialist in New York so I would be safe with the women I was with."

Charlie's eyebrows lift.

"I've told you how I was before you. You're the first female other than family to be here. I never fucked where I slept, and I never went back for seconds."

"Oh. Okay. But—"

"But you're different?" I question to see if we're on the same page.

She nods.

"Of course you are. You understand you're nothing like them, right? I didn't ask you to marry me because I screwed up and needed back in your panties. I've meant every word I've said to you. I love you. I'm in love with you and want to spend the rest of our lives together."

A smile spreads across her face.

"Me too."

It's my turn to nod. "The Daddy kink is hot as fuck with you. Honestly, I never did that in any serious way before because it wasn't my kink. With you, everything seems to be my kink, though."

"What was your kink, then?" she asks.

I open my Dom bag and extract my ropes. "Bondage, tying someone with rope. I'd like to try it with you."

"Like with me hanging from the ceiling?"

I laugh. "Eventually, yes. We'd need to have a setup at our place or join a safe club first, but to start, we can use my ropes and the bed."

Charlie's eyes heat. "Will you also blindfold me?"

I smirk because this woman could not be more perfect for me. "Do you want me to blindfold you?"

"I think it'll be better if you do. I'd like you to take all my control away. It's what I've been seeking without knowing. After the other day, I think this is what I might need to ground me again. Get me back into my body, if that makes sense."

"It makes perfect sense. I'm already in awe of you and honored that you're willing to give me this level of trust so fast, Kitten. Especially after I lied to you."

Charlie smiles and stands.

"Storm, stop. I forgive you. I don't love the idea of being lied to or omissions or truth which, in my book, are lies. But I understand why you felt you had to do what you did."

He pulls me into his arms and kisses me with such passion, my heart skips a beat.

Pulling back for air, I ask, "Should I be naked?"

"Ideally, but only if you'll be most comfortable that way. Tying you up doesn't need to involve sex."

"I think I'd like it to."

"Okay. Naked then."

Charlie works her clothing off while I ready my ropes and move the blankets out of the way. Situating the pillows where I'll need them, I turn to find Charlie standing bare before me.

My hand lowers to my raging cock, and I squeeze myself for relief. "Jesus, you are so fucking perfect."

I take her hand and return her to the edge of the mattress. "On your belly," I instruct.

Obeying my wishes, Charlie climbs on the bed, lying flat on her stomach.

I lift her hips and shove two pillows under them, then order, "Legs spread as far as comfortable, but I need to be able to tie them to the bed on either side."

Running a hand from her ankle to her calf, I lower my lips and kiss the muscle there, making her tremor slightly.

"Daddy?" she asks, not as a question, but to understand how this game is played.

"Yes, Kitten, call me Daddy while we play. And remember, if you need a safe word, if it gets too much and you need me to stop, use red. If you're just a little overwhelmed and need a break, use yellow. If I check in and ask if we're good, you'll tell me green. Understand?"

"Yes, Daddy."

I take her ankle into my grip again and stretch her leg a tad further before securing it to the bottom right of my bed. Checking she's tight and unable to move, but not at risk of damage to her nerves or ligaments, I ask, "Good?"

"Yes, Daddy," she obediently says. "Green."

"Good girl," I say as I plant a gentle kiss to the arch of her foot attached to my bed.

Turning my attention to her left leg, I repeat the process, then adjust her hips so her perfect pussy is on display.

"You look amazing already and I've only done half of your body. That pussy is so pretty and pink. Fucking wet for me already."

I run a finger through her wet folds, then bring it to rim her ass. "Maybe I'll take you here again tonight."

"Yes, Daddy, please."

I yank my shirt over my head as I curse and thank the powers above for bringing this woman into my life.

"Okay, let's get your arms situated. Fold your hands and clasp them together above your head. I'm going to tie them together then to the headboard."

I do exactly that and check in again to be sure she's secured and immobile but safe. Then I pull the black silk blindfold from my bag and straddle her back.

I place my palm gently on her chin and lift her face to mine, then lower to meet her lips. I kiss her with tongue and grind my cock through the slit of her ass.

The blindfold easily wraps around her head and shrouds her in sweet darkness.

"My voice, my scent, my touch," I say. "That's all you need to have. You know you have my heart, body, and soul. Now feel me, feel our connection with nothing in the way."

"Mmm." She hums, then her tongue jets out to lick the taste of me off her lips. "Please. More."

Needing relief and having the strongest desire to give her what she wants, I lower the zipper of my jeans and lose them and my briefs altogether so I can feel her wetness on my shaft.

I groan when I return my naked body and bare cock to hers. "Jesus fucking Christ, baby. You feel so good."

Running my length through her folds, I coat myself in her arousal before pulling back to look for the toy I need.

Finding the vibrating pleasure beads for her ass, I open the package and run them between my hands to warm them up. I add a dallop of lube and massage it into each of the four bubbly swells before popping them inside her.

"This is going to feel good, Kitten, but it's going to make holding off your climax very challenging, and Daddy needs you to be a good girl. Can you be a good girl for Daddy and not come until you're told?"

"I'll try, but—"

"I know, Spunky. This isn't going to be easy, but if you come, Daddy is going to have to punish you and that will take us longer to get to the best part."

"The—the best part?" she asks with a shaky voice.

"Yes. When I take the beads out one at a time and make you come with each one before I fuck your ass. Here we go."

The toy begins tiny at the tip, and I moan as the first bead smoothly penetrates her tight pucker and disappears into her darkest pleasure spots. The swells below the first graduate subtly in size and she groans under the fullness.

"How does that feel?"

"Full. Tight. Not like when you were there, but good."

"I'll be there soon enough to give it to you the way you want."

Soft and flexible, the beaded shaft bends and angles perfectly to contour with her shape.

Charlie arches under her restraints because I flip on the vibrations that blissfully run through her sensitive place to target her sweetest spots with ease. "Fuck!" she screams. "Storm, I can't—I'm going to come."

Crack.

I land my palm on the meaty flesh of her ass. "Don't you dare," I warn.

Charlie jolts at the unexpected sting from my palm and the harshness of my warning, her orgasm kept at bay.

"Good girl," I praise, my voice returning to the soft cadence she's used to. "Now, we're going to play a little. This isn't going to be easy on you, but I know you'll make me proud."

"I–I want that."

I dip a thick finger into her warm heat and her hips instantly buck and fall into rhythm with my pace. I'm careful not to give her the depth or the speed I know she prefers, so I can keep her dangling on the edge. But with a flick of my finger over her internal rough patch and an acceleration of the vibrations, I know Charlie may not ward off her climax for as long as I'd like.

She's still new to this type of play, so I ease up just in time.

I know it has the desired effect of edging when she cries out my name in frustration.

Her hips undulate, and Charlie tries for friction wherever she can find it.

I deliver another well-placed spank on her ass with a warning. "Keep trying to make yourself come instead of waiting for me to allow it, and you won't come for a month."

She gasps, but she also stills.

"That's right, baby. Your orgasms are mine, and I'll decide when you have them. Guessing you're not a fan of edging, huh?"

"Edging? Um, if that's what this is, then no. I want to come."

I chuckle and stroke my cock. "I know, me too, but give me a little longer. Deep breath in."

When she inhales, I impale her pussy with my dick.

From this position behind her, I'm deep. With the anal beads in place, she's extra tight and I remind myself to stay in my body so I'm not the one coming too soon.

I notch up the speed one more time on the beads and the vibrations grow so strong inside her, I feel them surge over my cock. Pulling out as quickly as I can, I grasp my base and squeeze to ward off my climax. "Fuck!"

"Yeah. I can't...stop. I can't stop. Fuck me, Daddy while I come."

I slam back inside her and by the second thrust, we come together so hard and loud, I'm thankful I won't have to face my neighbors ever again. Not that I really knew any of them, anyway.

I ride out our joint climax, then slowly leave her body.

But I'm not done with Charlie.

She still has the beads inside her, and I plan to give her an orgasm as I extract each one.

Lying on my back, I yank the pillow from under her and replace them with my face.

Charlie sputters some nonsense about me coming inside her, then licking her, but our joined flavor is already meeting the tip of my tongue as I suck her clit into my mouth and gently tug the first bead out.

"Yes!" Charlie cries as her body shakes from the surprise reaction and the orgasm that slams through her so shortly after her last.

"Three more," I mumble into her pussy.

"Oh, my god...No! No more. I can't come ag—"

I tug the second bead free and flick my tongue over her hardened bud before giving it a little nibble between my front teeth.

She comes again, but this time it's a dull throb I feel, not the hard pounding her body usually gives me.

"Okay, maybe these last two can come out together," I say as I pull the rest of the strand free, knowing when enough is enough.

Charlie collapses into a puddle of tears and sobs and I grab her up and cradle her into my arms, asking, "What? What's wrong? Tell me."

"I—I—I disappointed you. I gave up when you told me you wanted more."

I smile. Not because she's upset or because she wants to give me my way. I'm smiling because this woman is unbelievable and already seeks to find her pleasure wrapped in mine, the way mine is tied up in hers.

"Hey," I say as I run a soothing circle over her bare back. "Look at me." Turning her in my arms, I offer her that smile from a second ago. "You have made me so proud, Charlie. So proud."

"But—but I didn't come like you wanted."

"Baby, it's not about how many orgasms you have. It's about trust and this right here, wanting to please me as much as I want to make you happy. I love you with everything I have to give."

"I love you, too," she sobs, then lets me kiss her tears away as I gently rock into her body.

"Let me make love to you until we fall asleep."

Charlie

Storm and I returned to Lime Peak a few weeks ago and found the perfect compromise in our living arrangements. We both wanted to live together, but Storm's idea of what we required for comfort was a little beyond my means and I insisted on contributing to our household.

We both knew we didn't want to stay at the condo complex. As much fun as it had been to live near my friends and colleagues, starting a life together there just didn't feel right.

Storm wanted to look at the newest homes in the area or consider building from scratch. I wanted to check out the small cottages in Falls Village or maybe look at some in Waterland Isle.

We compromised on a home big enough for us to grow into over the next few years and landed on a fairly new development in Lime Peak. When the home at the very end of the cul-de-sac came on the market, we knew it was meant to be.

The back of the house has a view of the pond and the access to the trail is right there at the end of the quiet street.

With my busiest time of the year just ahead—planning for the summer camp, getting ready for the next academic calendar year, and hosting the part-time campers during their spring break—we were glad for a closing date at the start of summer. So until then, we moved his stuff into my condo and have been living in cramped style, blissfully happy ever since.

"Hey," Rourke calls as he enters my office. "I saw the summer lists. I'm glad Montana will be here."

I smile sadly at my friend and co-worker. "Yeah, me, too. I didn't want to push the issue with Jessie's parents, but they forced my hand at her annual review. She's near grade level. Graham Lowden, the principal from The Maritime Academy, has no issue with her attending there for classes, the public high school here is also fine with her attending there, and Jessie loved both places when Montana took her to visit."

"I hope we work it out in mediation. The last thing I want to do this summer is another due process hearing."

"I'm with you, but classes here with our population isn't what's in Jessie's best interest. She can go to The Maritime Academy in Falls Village or Lime Peak High School. Either way, she'll graduate with a diploma and might go to a community college for early childhood. There's no reason she couldn't be a teaching assistant at a daycare or in a preschool."

"Have you spoken to Hannah James?"

Hannah James owes Lollipop Preschool in Falls Village and lets us integrate our students there for an extended day program where they can spend time with mostly typically developing peers.

"Yeah, she's all for having her work there in the afternoons for two hours a day between school and dinner time. She'd have plenty of time for homework and if she wanted to do after-school activities, another option for some job experience outside of here, Silver Gardens, is also happy to have her. She enjoys working with the elderly as much as she does the little ones."

"Speaking of Silver Gardens, Jenny from The Perfect Pet called yesterday about coordinating our times with them. We're still sending the preschoolers over for the residents to read to, right?"

"Yes. Starting the first Wednesday of June and going through the last of August. Ruth from The Reading Nook is working with us, too. Is Jenny still good with coming over at the same time with the animals?"

"Yup. She just wanted to confirm the start date and that we all agreed on Wednesdays. She mentioned Tuesdays not being good because it was her photoshoot day with Beast."

I chuckle. Jenny's dog is social media famous for his pictures. "I'll have Neet call and set up a final meeting with all of us."

Rourke sits in the comfy chair he's claimed as his. "So, how are things with you and Storm?"

"Good, why?"

"No reason."

I eye him suspiciously because the way he asked leads me to believe there is a reason.

"Um, Brad and I are thinking of going away for a few weeks this summer. Just wondering if you and Storm made any plans?"

I stand abruptly. "Holy shit! Do you know something I don't?"

Storm has been acting a tad squirrelly lately, and I've been suspicious that it has something to do with us getting married. When we spoke about a date, I was noncommittal. Not because I didn't want to be his wife, but because with the camp in full swing during the summer, I was sort of hoping to have a wedding in the winter. It was also when we met, so it just feels like our season.

"No! Do you know something I don't?"

"Does Storm have something up his sleeve for this summer?"

Rourke takes too long to answer, which is my answer.

"Tell me right now or so help me god, I will assign you to middle school lunch duty for a month. When it's hot and they stink like barn animals who rolled in onions."

Rourke gags and holds up a hand. "Please. Anything but that. I'll tell you anything you want to know."

"Good. Start spilling."

After an earful from Rourke, my day goes by as every other except for one very important appointment, and I find myself back in my condo, alone by early evening. I'm tired, cold, and in need of a warm meal and a hot bath. Not necessarily in that order.

Before preparing dinner, I let the memories of days not long ago—before Storm entered my life—run through my head as I sit and enjoy a warm cup of tea on my sofa.

I realize now what I was missing.

Companionship between adults. Friendship between a man and a woman. Love between friends. Loyalty between lovers. A bond only trust can forge between a sexual Dominant man and a sexually submissive woman.

Before I'm too lost in my thoughts, the front door opens and on a whoosh of spring air, Storm joins me in the living room.

The savory aroma of something wonderful instantly fills the air around us and I sniff a deep inhale, then sigh when I know what he has in the bag.

"Hey Char," he says in greeting. "I brought you something."

Storm is the best man on the Earth.

"Oh yeah?" I play dumb, but my nose knows exactly what he's got in that bag.

"Yeah," he says with a sheepish grin on his handsome face. "Warm bread right out of Monte's oven and his famous chowder."

"Mmm." I moan, just thinking about the chunks of seafood and potatoes in the thick, creamy broth.

I follow him into the kitchen where he scoops us each a heaping bowl and places mine on the table with a hunk of hot, crusty bread before placing his across from where I've plopped down.

"Why don't you start in while I go grab my other surprise?"

"Another surprise?" I ask with a wiggle of my eyebrows. "Is this your way of asking for a threesome? Is there a guy waiting at the front door?"

Storm growls, then chuckles when I take a hunk of my bread and dip it into the savory broth, then moan when it hits my mouth. "God, the sounds you make go straight to my dick, but let's get one thing straight. Daddy doesn't share and if we were to have a threesome, that third party definitely wouldn't have a dick."

I give a fake pout, my lip sticking out while I shift around in my seat and Storm smirks, then says, "Behave while I run back out to the truck."

Returning, Storm has a pretty substantial box in his hands.

"You sure you didn't bring me a man?" I ask. "That box is enormous for your standard flowers and chocolate, which," I spoon a little more chowder into my mouth, then swallow, "has me wondering if these surprises have anything to do with you fucking up again."

"I didn't fuck up. I don't have plans on ever fucking up with you again. Those few days when you weren't speaking to me were the worst of my life, and I've had some pretty shitty days. Hell, I've been shot, and that wasn't even as bad."

He hands me a large box that wiggles in my hands.

Storm and I discussed lots of things over the last few weeks after I said yes to his proposal of marriage, children and pets being amongst them.

Opening the box, I find a white Persian kitten and a black lab puppy staring up at me.

"Oh, my god!" I exclaim. "They are so cute."

Putting the box on the floor, I take them out, one in each hand, and cuddle them to my chest. Looking at Storm, I give him a glare. We talked about pets. We didn't say we were getting one, let alone two. And especially not now. We won't be in our home anytime soon and then there's the surprise I have for him.

"I know," he defends. "I know, but I was at Elliot's with the guys in—"

"That damn mancave. Yeah, I figured."

Storm laughs. "Yes, in the mancave. As I was saying, Lucas was there, and he was going on and on about this puppy and kitten he and Jenny just took in and how they're inseparable and it's so cute watching them together. Then someone said we should go see them. I think it was Ace, because he only acts like a badass, but he's really a fucking pussy. Anyway, he talked us into going to The Perfect Pet to see these two and I couldn't help myself."

"Do they have names?"

"No. You can—"

Kissing their heads one at a time, I say. "Salt and Pepper."

A smile covers Storm's face. "We aren't naming our children after spices, are we?"

"Well, that depends," I say, laying a hand on my belly.

Storm's eyes widen. "Are you trying to tell me something?"

He pulls me into his arms, the puppy and kitten squished between us.

"I was late, so I went to my doctor today. I was going to wait for a grand gesture idea to hit me and tell you like all these women do on social media. But when Rourke and I were talking today, he may have let it slip—"

"Or you threatened him with middle school lunch duty in the heat of summer."

My mouth drops open. "How did—"

"He called to warn me."

"I hate you both."

Letting me go because Salt and Pepper protest the sandwich we made with them in the middle, I bend down and deposit them on the floor.

Sitting next to them, Storm joins me, then tugs me onto his lap. "And..." he prompts.

"Well, I got the sense that you were planning a surprise wedding for me, and I had this surprise for you. It felt too much like us not telling each other stuff, so..."

"So, what are you telling me?"

"That I'm not going to be the only one calling you Daddy soon."

Storm's lips crash over mine, then I feel the smile that splits his face as he asks, "How? When?"

Pulling back, I say, "After the kidnapping. I missed my pill a few nights, then totally forgot when we were together in the forest. It was so romantic and I missed you so much. It totally slipped my mind and then I thought maybe it was okay. But when I was late, I got worried you'd be mad, so I wanted to know for sure before I—"

Storm kisses me again. This time, his tongue forces my mouth open, and he sweeps inside to taste me. With a moan, I twirl my tongue with his as his hands twine into my hair.

Breathlessly, I say, "We can't leave them to have sex. What if they pee in the house or get scared all alone?"

A wicked smile spreads across his handsome face. "Jenny gave me everything we'll need. I'll run out to the truck really quick for the crate and we can be like my brother and Lainey and fuck in the kitchen. They'll close their eyes."

With that, Storm runs out the front door and I laugh as I herd our new growing family into my lap and wait for the typical Roland debauchery to begin.

"Daddy's a kinky man, guys," I warn. "Better get used to it."

About Kitty Berry

Kitty Berry grew up an only child who never wished for a sibling in a small town in Connecticut. After graduating with a degree in Education, she began teaching in the field and raised a family. Her literary influences happened later in life when she stumbled upon contemporary romance.

Being a creative person by nature who came into writing during a time in her life when the busy balance of career and family made her crave an escape, Kitty took that desire and turned it into a second career.

In 2013, she published her first novel from The Stone Series, *Sliding*. Since then, she has written ten other novels in that series, including a holiday edition released in late 2018. In 2019, Berry released a trilogy titled *The Anatomy of Love*, along with a carry-over novel, *Vines of Ivy*. She released the *Compatible Companions Trilogy* the following year. 2021 saw the conclusion of her *Falls Village Collection*, which is an anthology hybrid she created. After that, Kitty released a duet (Blossom Springs). She was part of an anthology for the TNT-NYC Author Signing Event in 2022 and turned her stand-alone Rom-Com titled *Burden of Proof* into a full-length novel. She is currently working on *The Romance Through the Year* holiday novellas and her new Lime Peak Series.

Kitty founded RomantiConn (a romance author signing event annually held in CT) in 2019 that she attends along with others on the east coast.

Visit   Kitty's   website   @ http://www.kittyberryauthor.com

Made in the USA
Middletown, DE
15 April 2023

28770675R00136